# THE
# DAYMAKER

# THE
# DAYMAKER

## Ann Halam

Orchard Books
A division of Franklin Watts, Inc.
New York & London

ORCHARD BOOKS
387 Park Avenue South
New York, New York 10016
*Orchard Books Canada*
20 Torbay Road
Markham, Ontario 23P 1G6
Orchard Books is a division of Franklin Watts, Inc.

Manufactured in the United States of America
Book design by Jennifer Campbell

10 9 8 7 6 5 4 3 2 1

The text of this book is set in Linotron 11 on 14 point Sabon

*Library of Congress Cataloging-in-Publication Data*
Halam, Ann.
The daymaker.
Summary: Endowed with mystical powers, young Zanne takes a journey in search
of the mysterious "daymaker" in order to become a full-fledged covenor.
[1. Fantasy]
PZ7.H1283Day   1987   [Fic]   87-5813
ISBN 0-531-05710-0
ISBN 0-531-08310-1 (school and library)

# CHAPTER 1

THERE WAS NO moon. Toward morning a waning crescent of silver would rise over Inland's eastern borders; until then the frostbright stars were alone. Snow had been falling, and the stars looked down on a landscape of little fields and little woods: all white and silent, wrapped in the sleep of winter.

But the stillness was not complete. There was a shifting stain on the white coverlet. A band of riders moved in furtively, with a blue glint of weapons, toward an isolated cluster of small homesteads. Luckily, the people of this countryside knew what they had to fear at the dark of the moon at this season. Life might seem very safe and peaceful in this quiet land. But in fact danger was never very far away....

Zanne's mother came in from the snow. Her big coat, which reached to her ankles, was crusted with it. The children were curled up by the kitchen stove. There were chores undone: it was a very cold night, and the kitchen was a seductive haven. Mother hadn't taken her boots off in the porch—something you must always do. Snow dropped from them onto the bright rag rug that covered the middle of the stone floor, which Zanne loved because of its colors, and its magical

5

warmth to small bare feet. The little girl saw patches of black dampness growing out of her mother's white footprints. She knew someone was in bad trouble.

"Kila," said Zanne's mother, "wrap yourself up. And the others. Leave the lamps. A dark house would only attract them."

Kila was Father's apprentice, who had come to live with Zanne's family while she learned to be a weaver. Without a word she ran for the coat cupboard. Father had come in behind mother. He was looking around the kitchen as if he'd never seen it before. Mother was clearing off the farm desk, putting some things in a chest and others into the massive immovable desk itself. For Zanne the friendly yellow lamplight disappeared and appeared again as she was thrust into garments, and every time it reappeared something stranger was going on.

"Run," said Mother, and the three children ran, down the bumpy red tiles into the old dairy: the oldest part of the house, a storeroom now. Father and Mother stood at the door. They were holding long stakes split and bound into tines at the head—pitchforks. What on earth could that be for, in the snow?

Zanne was going to ask her father, but he hugged her just then, and for some reason the familiar soft scrub of his beard frightened her into silence. Mother held Kila at arm's length and touched her on the forehead, on the mouth, on the cusp of her collarbones; making little circles with her finger.

Zanne and Bren, her brother, ran to a row of tiny windows set deep in the old dairy's outer wall. They huffed hot breath on the glass, and through the white scratchings of frost saw an extraordinary sight. At the bottom of the farm track, where it met the road to the village, was a crowd of wildfire flares; orange and yellow in the blue-black and snowy darkness. As they watched, two more flares, with bouncing

6

shadows under them, came hurrying down and joined the rest.

"Come away from there," said Kila. "We've got to keep quiet and not show a light."

It was deathly cold. Zanne fell asleep and woke up with her cheek squashed painfully on the chest of precious books and papers. She remembered that her mother had not kissed her and made up her mind to cry.

But then something warm brushed her chin. It was the rag rug, that her mother had bundled after them with the chest. It snuggled itself around her, as if someone was tucking her up in bed. When Zanne closed her eyes she could still see the kindly colors. She burrowed her cold nose down and fell asleep again, comforted.

That was a bitter winter. The worst in living memory for the people of Garth, and probably for the whole of Inland. There was fierce discussion at every Covenant meeting over the problem of the raiders. In other parts depredations were more common. Garth was not usually impressed by tales of woe from the tradestowns—the loss of luxuries that should never have been piled up in the first place. It was different when the trouble reached so far as home.

It was the custom of Inland people to make a harvest assessment every year, and each household would give exactly what it could afford in kind or in trade: the dole to be sent in wagons to the border and left there for the miserable outlaws. If the outlaws thought that this was a tribute exacted by terror, let them. It was not; it was charity. Some people said the harvest dole must be too low; otherwise there would be no raiding. Some said it should be cut down to teach the raiders a lesson.

But all this passed over Zanne's head as she daydreamed through the meetings or engaged in surreptitious pinching battles with Bren. She had no foreknowledge of the part those adventurers from the Outlands were to play in her life. By summertime (it was the summer she was four years old) she had almost forgotten the night they slept in the dairy. And that was the last hard winter for several years. Garth relapsed into its habitual sleepy peace.

On three sides the fields of Garth were bounded by wooded hills. To the west, beyond Townsend Farm where Zanne lived, the bare sheep downs rolled away into blue distance. Once there had been a city here, long ago when Inland was a very different place. But hardly any trace remained now of "the land of the towers of light": only a few fragments turned up by the plow or a couple of odd shaped boulders standing in the corner of a field.

Zanne and her brother and the other Garth children played at "cities" but they didn't really know what the word meant. The world to them was the seven farms of Garth, with their bean rows and plow and orchard and pasture. Townsend, Upper Valley, Bine End, Eastcot, Shorthouse, Longhill, and Low.

It was a small settlement, not big enough for tradespeople. Some of the farms had crafts attached to them by tradition: the pottery kiln at Bine End, the carpentry shop at Low. Other skills came to the valley when tradesfolk married into the farming families or when children were apprenticed out and brought their learning home. But the nearest shops and streets were a long day's journey away at Mosden, the tradestown, and Zanne hardly ever saw them.

Sometimes she tried to imagine the towers of light: great bars of gold and silver as tall as the hills, marching away, away as far as Mosden. But she could never make the picture real; it was always just a copy of what sunlight looks like coming through rifts in a cloud.

"Why can't I imagine it?" she asked her mother.

And Mother said, "Because that world is gone, Zanne.

8

Inland is here instead. And your mind, that imagines, is part of Inland."

Zanne didn't understand, but she was satisfied. What Mother said was always satisfying then, even when it was very mysterious.

The village of Garth itself consisted only of the meetinghouse with its wooden belltower, the Garth Inn for less serious meetings, and a row of pensions—little cottages belonging to six old women and five old men who had retired from their farms. The Garth Inn family looked out for them and they in turn looked out for any indigent strangers, tended the meetinghouse, and taught Garth children old tales and useful skills (when they could catch them).

Zanne's father, Hurst, was a weaver. He had been born at the tradestown of Mosden, twenty vales away. As a young man he had traveled the roads with his trade. Now he stayed at home at Townsend and the young came to him to learn.

Townsend was a low, white, L-shaped house, set with its outhouses in a neat stone-walled yard. It was a prosperous holding. The big kitchen was hung (when raiders were not expected) with beautiful, richly colored cloths, most of them born on Hurst's big loom that stood in the wide sun-filled loft chamber overhead. Zanne's little room was in that loft too. Conferred on her with great ceremony when she was five, it had blue curtains with red apples woven into them, and a quiltcover of green grass and yellow buttercups. However, Garth was a strong covenanting valley, and Zanne lived a strict life as a child. She ate bean porridge and bread and honey, little milk or butter, and meat only a few days in the year. She used an earth privy, and water came from the kitchen pump. At night, unless Zanne's mother was working at her desk, by two hours after sunset the valley was dark from the downs to the river Moss.

Zanne's mother, Arles, was Garth's covener. She led the

speakers at those endless meetings when Zanne dozed on the children's bench at the back. Zanne didn't mind the meetings. In the summer she watched the swallows, flitting in and out of the air slats and making butterfly shadows over the whitewashed roof space. In the winter she tried to get a bench end by the stove, where she could read the names on the wall. There was her grandmother, Paris Cutler, who had died in a bad raid years and years ago. And her grandfather, Negan Townsend, whom she could just about remember. There were great-grandparents and great-great-great as well, but they had been washed over by now. So many layers of names wrapped around Garth meeting. It was a comfortable, safe feeling.

Before the child was old enough for work or lessons, Arles Townsend would often take Zanne in front of her on her pony, on covenanting calls. When the milk was due to go into Mosden, in churns of sycamore wood, or the bales of wool at fleece harvest, Arles and Zanne went down to the wagon road to wish it well. If there was meat to be killed or a tree to be downed, or if a swathe of badland needed sweetening, Zanne's mother would be called out to the farms. Sometimes she was called to a sick animal, a failed crop, or a difficult birth or death, animal or human. But that was rare. Garth people kept the Covenant, and so no harm could come to them. Zanne knew that.

Children were not supposed to watch a meat killing, but of course they had to. Zanne would crouch in the barn with the farm's own offspring and peep through the swatches while her mother took a sheep between her knees as if she was going to strip its wool.

*Sister, don't blame me*, she said (or brother). *I will die too, and be eaten.* Arles' strong hands closed under the animal's narrow chocky jaws—and it was limp and gone. People grumbled that Arles Townsend was too plainspoken. She

10

ought to use some decent long words. The old covener used to say "consumed"—not common munching "eaten."

But though Zanne giggled with her friends because it seemed the thing to do, she listened to the grownups and she knew they were wrong. Her mother must be doing it right, because Zanne could feel inside her what happened when the sheep went limp. There was a light like a candle flame. It shook and nearly went out, but mother's hands kept it steady.

Zanne was a good child. She did her lessons and she did her chores: including the outwork that everybody shared— clearing stones out of plowland, the horrible potato picking and other more pleasant harvests. She had one marked peculiarity, as little children will, and that was her delight in anything that went up and down or round and round. Even when she was teething as a baby, she never cried if she could watch her father at his loom. Hurst hoped she would be a weaver.

But it turned out the attraction was more general. She was equally entranced by any tool that moved. The greatest treat you could give her was to take her to Mosshole, down the river, and let her watch the water mill where the flour of three valleys was ground. Some of Zanne's friends told her it was wrong for a covener's daughter to visit the Mill family. Zanne hadn't the least idea why. Mother only laughed. She said the parents of those children were welcome to go back to the quern, if they had so much time on their hands.

Zanne loved all her family (except Bren occasionally) and nearly everyone in Garth. But most of all she loved her uncle Lol. He was her mother's brother—a round faced young man with yellow hair and gray eyes like mother and Zanne. Years ago he had taken his share out of the farm; he preferred a wandering life. Still there was always room at Townsend for him, and sometimes he stayed for months. When he

11

was in residence, children were drawn to Townsend yard like wasps to an orchard full of windfalls. He was never too busy or too tired to make toys for them or invent games.

Zanne's father had traveled, but his storytelling was pitiful compared to Lol's. Uncle Lol had been a horse trader, a wandering player, a peddler. His past was full of daring ventures, narrow escapes, and strange twists of fate. He wore a bright green jacket with gold braid on the collar for everyday, and breeches to match instead of knitted leggings like the country people. Hurst Weaver called his wife's brother "flash Lolly" and fingered the cloth of that suit with disdain.

Sometimes Lol committed crimes (like the time he was caught teaching some young people how to make a whisky still). Arles said, "Brother or no brother, next time you need to go to earth dig yourself a hole and jump in it." But Lol knew (as he told Bren and Zanne) how to lie low and let the storm pass over. He always came back. And his wickedness just made Zanne love him more.

There was one thing about Uncle Lol more wonderful than all the rest. He could do magic. He was careful with this skill outside the house, because the people of Garth did not approve of such trickery. But when Zanne was a baby he would put her into fits of laughter by making her beechwood platter grow eyes and mouth and pull faces at her through her dinner. When she got older he would draw pictures that came alive, make her yellow hair crackle with colored fire; turn an apple she was eating into a bird that pecked her nose and flew away. Once there was an egg that talked when she pulled it out from under her own hen Blackie.

"Don't blame me, sister," she mumbled, groping in the warm straw still half asleep.

"I don't blame you," piped up the egg cheerfully. "Everybody's got to go sometime!"

12

It could not be eaten. Zanne kept it in a box until the yolk rattled like a stone inside, and for years she thought she could still hear it muttering sometimes.

Kila was almost grown up by now. Soon she would leave them for her first trade journey. Men don't make magic, she declared. They only make fools of themselves. But for Bren and Zanne the fun Lol provided was real and wonderful. Especially for Zanne because she discovered she could do magic tricks herself.

Hurst was concerned. He was afraid Lol's tuition would do Zanne lasting harm. But Arles told him not to worry.

"I was the same when I was that age," she said.

Perhaps part of her tolerance was the comfort of seeing her scapegrace brother almost respect himself again, in the admiration of this golden-bright, loving child.

Lol vanished and returned, sometimes not seen from one year's end to the next. In Garth valley the seasons slipped by placidly. There were occasional alarms around Dark and Year's End, but no raids that reached as far as Garth, safe as it was in the heart of Inland. There were good harvests and less good harvests; the Covenant meeting argued as always about different weather needs. Zanne at pensioner school chanted the months with her friend Loyse Bine End: First Moon, Second Moon, Trime, New Spring. Old Spring, New Summer, Midsummer, Oldsummer. Sunfall, Leafall, Old Moon, Dark. Year's End and then First Moon ... She grew up to be ten years old in absolute freedom (though she didn't believe so) and so happy that she rarely even thought of the word.

It was New Summer, sheep-stripping time. Any day now the flocks would come off the downs and stamp boldly into their own farmyards, pricking their ears and bleating for attention. At stripping time the heavy fleeces were ready to drop like autumn leaves. There were always a few lazy beasts

13

who stayed up on the hill, letting their wool fall anywhere. The young people went after those; it was an excellent excuse for sweethearting.

Zanne was in the woods. She was alone for a change and enjoying the sensation. She was following the track of a broad ride between the trees covered only by thin scrawny turf and weeds. There were patches of this badland in Garth valley. Some farmers broke them up with picks and shovels and called in Arles Townsend to sweeten the soil. Others preferred to leave them to "come back" in their own time. Children found the patches fascinating because of the treasure that might be discovered. There was rarely anything whole, just tantalizing fragments of glass and colored crockery; but the promise was enough. Zanne walked with her head down, poking hopefully wherever tree roots had broken up the rock-hard undersurface.

This ride was different from the bad patches in that it was going somewhere. Out of Garth, far away. Zanne's uncle Lol had told her rides like these were old, old roads. If you followed them they would lead you back into the past. Into the land of the towers of light. In that land every house had a tree outside it that grew stars instead of flowers. Everybody lived on meat and sugar candy, and little children didn't have to work. They had nothing to do but read story books and play at puzzles all day. In that land, things were made of neither wood nor stone nor skin, nor metal out of the rock . . . Zanne didn't swallow these tales whole anymore, the way she used to. She knew the answer to that Inland riddle. If you count plants as wood—then that was the land of nothing and nowhere. But she enjoyed the story telling still.

She had walked a long way from Garth, maybe a vale or two. A vale was the Inland measure of distance, but it wasn't an exact quantity. Twenty vales was about as far as you

14

could expect to go by wagon in a day if nothing went wrong—as far as Mosden. Zanne had seen "maps" copied in her mother's books, but there were no maps of Inland as far as she was aware. And so no one knew exactly where Mosden was, or Garth either. . . . They were where you found them.

Perhaps the time that people called the lost past, the time of the towers of light, was like that too. Not even Mother could tell you exactly how many years it was since the shining towers fell. Perhaps that was like asking how long is a vale. The past is where you find it. I wonder, thought Zanne, if I keep on walking will it really be there, just like Mosden?

Zanne liked ideas like that and often played with them in her mind. But treasure seeking was giving her a crick in the neck. She abandoned it and wandered into the green shade of the great Garth beeches, her feet shush-shushing in last year's leaves. She found her way to a small tributary of the Moss, sat down, and dabbled her feet in the cool dark water. It was very quiet in the beechwood. Zanne contemplated her bare toes, fattened and pallid in the magnifying stream. She wished she had a pair of shoes to wear in summer. Her feet were never quite hard enough to scuff and kick without getting bruised. She had cracked a toenail now, treasure hunting. But the covener's children are always the meanest raised; she had heard people say so. If Mother could tell people when to kill and when not to kill, then obviously she had to be at least as strict at Townsend.

She didn't have murderous designs on any of the five Townsend cows; or Mother's covenanting pony, or Hazel and Rowan, the two great gentle oxen. But she thought it would be a good idea to trade for leather, the way they had traded for the real glazed crockery they used on meeting days. Father had explained to her why this wouldn't be right,

15

it would be just the same as tanning an uncovenanted hide themselves. Zanne was not convinced.

She decided to make herself a pair of shoes out of beech leaves. The dead ones looked quite like leather. It was easy enough. But she couldn't get rid of the crackle. She felt silly and let the shoes go.

Zanne could do better tricks than that. For years now she'd been able to do anything Uncle Lol could show her, and often she teased him, instead of the other way round. Like the time she made him see a wolf on the stairs. He was really scared, but he couldn't stop seeing it even when he knew it was Zanne playing a trick on his mind. Mother laughed and laughed. But she said to Zanne, "Don't you ever do anything like that to another child," in such a tone that Zanne never did.

Uncle Lol told her that she was an "infant prodigy" and that she was the best illusion-merchant he had ever met. But Zanne was beginning to wonder if she was growing out of magic. She knew the things she did weren't real, however impressive, and it got boring to see people being fooled. Still more boring to fool yourself. Besides, from the looks she caught sometimes when she was playing tricks, she was sure her mother and father had started to disapprove.

This was sad, because magic was her only skill. No one seemed to think she had talent for any other trade. Bren was the first born and he would farm Townsend. What would Zanne do? In consideration of her future she had recently proposed marriage to her friend Mir of Upper Valley. He could take up a trade and she would farm. That would be best. And yet, there seemed to be something lacking....

Uncle Lol had not been home for months. She hoped he would come back soon. She was old enough by now to know Garth people didn't like him much. Perhaps he was finally tired of their grudging welcome and had decided to stay

16

away forever. Even Father didn't want Lol at Townsend. But there was no magic in Father. Nor in Mother either.

"Boring stay-at-homes," muttered Zanne. "I'll die if Uncle Lol doesn't come back."

Thinking about her uncle, wishing for him, she wasn't surprised when she looked into the stream and distinctly saw Uncle Lol's face instead of her own. They were alike after all. She was the one who took after the Townsends. Father and Bren were long and thin in the face, with brown eyes and hair. It was some moments before she realized this was not a daydream but an actual sending: a very daring kind of magic Lol had just begun to teach her last autumn, making her swear not to tell her mother.

"Woo-ee!" yelled Zanne, jumping to her feet.

She charged through the wood, forgetting her bruised toe. She knew he couldn't be far away. The sending was coming from somewhere up along the ride. She raced toward it, hurdling over clumps of nettles. Home for the sheep stripping! That was just like Lol, Father would say. He could smell free beer across the breadth of Inland.... She wondered as she hurtled along why he was not on the wagon road. It was not like Uncle Lol to go on foot if he could cadge a lift, or travel rough when he could travel smooth.

It was the smell of smoke that saved her. She wasn't alarmed. The wood was by no means dried out after a rather slow, damp spring. She was only puzzled as to how the fire could have started. She slowed down, peering around, and so did not race straight into the middle of the raiders' camp.

They were occupying a clearing right on the barren ride. There were fifty people or more: women, men—a few who looked not much older than Bren. They were sitting around a bonfire. There was a crowd of horses; saddled and bridled, hobbled in pairs or tied to low branches. Zanne gaped. A delectable smell reached her nostrils, mingled with the

17

woodsmoke. These people were eating meat. They wore boots, and clothes all decorated with metal and leather and beads.

The little girl stared in bewilderment. She had never seen such riches. No one used a saddle or a bitted bridle in Garth. The Covenant pony's halter was rope with wooden rings. The smoky devouring flames fascinated her. Fire, wild fire, was a treat for special occasions in Zanne's world. Or else a tool used with strict care.

Gradually it dawned on her that this must be a gang of raiders. For it was only in Uncle Lol's stories that the old road would lead you back to the past. In real life, as Zanne well knew, these rides led out eventually into the badlands, the Outlands, where the raiders came from. Zanne had heard the Outlands called "desert places." She couldn't imagine a place where nothing grew. She thought of a plowed field, like a brown bare hem stitched round the edge of Inland.

She had only the vaguest memory of that snowy night when she was four years old. But like all Inland children she had learned quite a lot about these human wolves and their ways.

Raiders don't come in summer, thought Zanne.

She was hiding behind a tree. It was only by luck that no one had spotted her as she came running up. Raiders don't come in summer, she repeated to herself. Zanne had a habit of leaping to excited conclusions, which she wished she could control. She was a proud child; she didn't like it when people laughed at her. It would be horrible if she were to run home yelling and then find there was a perfectly reasonable explanation for all this, known to everybody but daydreaming Zanne.

Then she saw Uncle Lol. She had forgotten about the sending until that moment. There he was on the edge of the feast, his yellow hair tousled in his eyes and dead leaves on the shoulders of his jacket. It was the blue suit that had replaced his green one, equally braided and flashy. He looked more ordinary with the outlaws. In Garth people hardly ever wore bright colors, even on holidays. Uncle Lol was a prisoner! At once Zanne's usual confidence returned. She stepped back from the beech bole and dropped to her hands and knees.

A few minutes later she was as close to him as she could be, and none of the armed guards posted around the clearing had spotted her. She tried to send to him, but either she failed or Lol was too distracted to recognise the touch of magic. The raiders were engrossed in their meal. She hissed, unmagically; he saw her and his face lit up. He managed to move a bit farther from the fire.

"Zanne, you sweet child. You've saved my life!"

"Lucky they didn't tie you up," whispered Zanne. "This is the plan. You run for it. I'm going to stampede the horses."

Uncle Lol looked tired. She noticed that the braid around his collar was worn down to string in places. His hands were greasy from eating meat with his fingers. He laughed, a breathless little laugh, and cast a quick glance over his shoulder.

"No need for that, lassie. We're all friends here."

I've made a fool of myself, thought Zanne. But she didn't understand, because Uncle Lol was definitely frightened.

"But you *sent* to me. Don't you want to be rescued?"

"I didn't—" began Uncle Lol, and broke off looking at Zanne sharply.

Then he smiled, his eyes lighting up again.

"Never mind. You've saved my liver and lights anyway. I want you to do something—only you must be quick."

"All right. What is it?"

"You know the chest that lives under the farm desk?"

"With mother's books in it?"

19

"That's the one. Bring me the books, Zanne. Whatever you can carry. Put them in a bag, bring them out here. I—er—I owe these friends of mine some money...."

Zanne had never seen coined money in her life. She stared at her uncle blankly, but inside her stomach was shrinking into a small cold stone. Behind him, she could see that the meal was over. Booted feet were carelessly kicking the fire apart. People were bringing up horses. Zanne saw the crossbows and throwing spears stowed in saddle holsters. Lol scrubbed his fingers through his hair, leaving trails of grease. He laughed again, guiltily, helplessly.

"Zanne, be a good child and do as you're told. I'll stall them here ... I had to tell them, you see. They're a rough crowd. Please get the books. Otherwise—I don't know what...."

She could not speak. When she ran it was from his face, with its weak terrified smile.

It was only when her breath started catching painfully that she realized how far she was from home. The raiders were on horseback. She plunged to her knees, clasped her hands and gabbled, "Under the Covenant, beech trees lend me your strength...." Sometimes when she said the Covenant, the candle flame in Zanne flared so bright it ought to show through her skin. Nothing like that happened now. She just kept running, running, until at last she passed the pension cottages at a painful trot and stumbled up the belltower steps. She grabbed the rope, and the bell pealed out dementedly. It was never used except as an alarm. The covener didn't need its aid to call her meeting. People came running up.

"Raiders!" sobbed Zanne. "Raiders in the woods!"

There was no need by then for anyone to try and make out her story. Another settlement farther up river had been

20

warned by the foresters and sent word by road. If Zanne had not escaped early from her chores to go off alone she would have been kept indoors. The children of Lower Garth, and Zanne, went into the meetinghouse undercroft with the frailest pensioners.

The mouth of Garth valley was narrow and stopped up with sturdy defenders. These strict covenanters possessed nothing that could be used only as a weapon, but they knew how to handle their farm tools. Everybody wanted to know why this pest had appeared so far out of season, but then the raiders themselves appeared and halted discussion for a while. Outlaws were on the edge of their range here. An attack was never sustained; it was like a flash flood— damaging and dangerous but soon over. The valley boasted twenty-two adults able to fight and six flores, the Inland name for young people who were no longer children. With the Covenant's protection, that was plenty for defense.

By the Covenant Inland people had promised to live at peace with all creatures of the natural world. The Garth villagers had the goodwill of the ground they tilled, a will that didn't show itself in any spectacular way but which worked for them nevertheless. And though the raiders were outside the Covenant, their horses were not. Covener Arles shouted to the beasts, reminding them. The horses became unmanageable when their riders tried to force the defenders' line. (Raiders used to plundering deep within Inland would have left the animals in the forest.) That was almost the end. The band broke up and retreated, leaving five of their number badly hurt and one dead. But it was a long, hot, bloody, frightening afternoon.

Zanne stepped into the kitchen at Townsend. The big room was cool and shadowy. In summer its fat earthenware stove was cold to the touch except at cooking times; the sun heat her mother had coaxed there like a swarm of bees sunk down to a sleepy core. Out in the valley everyone was busy putting out fires the raiders had started in Bine End's uncut meadows, and tending the wounded. She had sneaked away, hugging her awful secret.

The faded rag rug had blood on it. She looked at the splotches dully. There had been no fighting up here. She knew, after a moment, whose blood it was.

She found him in the old dairy. He was hiding behind a pile of lumber, his back against the cobwebby wall. Zanne's lamp showed his round merry face turned haggard, with lines of terror drawn dark on cheesy white. She looked at him and knew this was what happened in the stories. She was seeing Uncle Lol the way he looked when he was having a narrow escape, in a daring venture. There was a dark wet patch on his forearm; he was holding onto it with his other hand.

"I didn't tell," she said hoarsely.

"They'll find out. Your mother's going to kill me."

His eyes pleaded with her.

"I've got no food. I'm hurt."

On the floor beside him was an awkward bundle. Zanne knew that he had come back to Townsend not to confess to the harm he'd done but to grab whatever he could carry. He wasn't going to be able to come home again this time. She picked up the bundle. He let her take it without a word, which was horrible.

"Hide in the split oak," she said. "I'll have to wait until everyone's asleep but I'll come."

The split oak stood in Home Meadow, just below the farmyard gate. It had been struck by lightning long ago but had survived and grown old and massive. Generations of Townsend children had used the riven hollow in its low crown as a refuge. She put Father's silver candlesticks back up above the stove and Mother's books back in the chest. She

22

was only just in time. As she shut the chest lid, she heard the yard gate bang. She was sitting up at the kitchen table when Mother came in. Zanne trembled, twisting her hands in her lap under the table. Mother looked at the bloodstained rug.

"Zanne," said Arles gently. "Don't be frightened, but tell me the truth. Have you seen your uncle Lol today?"

"No."

Mother sighed. "Zanne, he brought the raiders here."

"How do you know that?" cried Zanne, shaking all over.

"They told us so. We have five of the poor devils laid out in the meetinghouse. Lol brought them here. He promised his friends there was treasure in Garth and he could help them to it. . . . Don't break your heart, darling. He probably thought he could weasel a way out before it came to fighting."

There were hot tears falling on Zanne's hands. Mother crossed the room and tried to hug her, but Zanne ducked away.

"He isn't here!"

When she looked up, the kitchen was empty.

Bren and Kila and Hurst came home. Kila was shaken and tired. She was seventeen and had been in the fighting. But they went out again almost immediately. They were helping to search the valley for Lol Townsend.

Zanne lay on her bed. She felt ill. She felt as if someone was punching her in the stomach. No one would find Lol. Zanne had known for years how to make the oak tree hide her so that people walked by and never thought she might be there. It wasn't exactly magic, not like Lol's clever tricks, but it never failed. Only how long, how long would the light last?

Suddenly she sat up. She could hear Mother and Father talking down in the yard.

"He's been there all the time," said her mother's voice wearily. "I didn't know he was capable of hiding himself from me—that's why I missed him." A murmur from Father.

"Go indoors, Hurst Weaver. I have not the meeting's approval. You shouldn't be involved. He is my brother."

Zanne's window was unglazed. The shutter was open. She looked out and saw Mother crossing the yard, carrying the bag that usually held her covenant tools. She heard Lol's terrified whisper again.

"Your mother's going to kill me—"

The split oak stretched its branches low and straight. Its leaves brushed the meadow grass, green margined with gold in the evening sunlight. Zanne ran after her mother. The hiding trick was broken. She must do something more. Lol couldn't help himself. She knew that. He could make an apple turn into a bird and fly out of your hand; but when you looked down the bitten apple would be rolling away, and the bird had vanished. It wasn't real, it was just fooling ... No magic then. She stopped at the yard gate and clasped her hands: *under the Covenant ... under the Covenant ...*

"Lol, come down from there."

When her brother did not appear, Arles jumped up without ceremony onto the broadest of the oak's three low boughs and peered into the hollow crown. She got down again. He was there, she knew it. Men who make magic only make fools of themselves. Still, she had never had the heart to take her brother's small talent away from him. He had little enough to be proud of. Now she was horrified to find that her weak, treacherous brother had somehow become as powerful as any covener in Inland. He would have to be, to hide from Arles Townsend. Grimly, remorsefully, she set out to break him.

The oak tree shivered through all its great bulk, the meadow grass lay down flat as if under a storm of hail. There was a crack like thunder. Hurst and Kila and Bren came running out of the kitchen. And there was Lol made visible inside the split oak's trunk, with the corded bark running through his body and his yellow hair pulled up and grown into the wood. His mouth and eyes were stretched wide in terror.

Arles stared. Then she turned around. Little Zanne was standing at the yard gate, shaking all over and looking as frightened as Lol.

"Zanne," she said, as if speaking to someone standing on the edge of a high cliff. "Can you let him go?"

The little girl shook her head dumbly.

"Give him to me then. Under the Covenant. . . . "

Lol collapsed in a heap on the grass. Arles waited without speaking until he got to his feet. She handed him the covenanting bag.

"That's what we can spare," she said. "Be careful. The meeting is looking for you. And some of your 'friends' may still be about, outside my holding."

Zanne watched Uncle Lol walk away, up the sloping meadow, with the bag of food and clothes clutched in his arms. He vanished over the brow, and with him went the first unclouded sunlight of her childhood.

Arles Townsend came to her daughter. She made the sign of the Covenant, the magical O of creation, on the little girl's forehead and on her mouth and on the cusp of her collarbones, all the while with an expression in her eyes that told Zanne she was in bad, bad trouble.

"Zanne, how long have you been able to do magic of that kind?"

Zanne was crying. She did not understand what had happened, except that her Uncle Lol was gone forever. Worse than gone. It was as if the Uncle Lol she loved had never existed.

"It wasn't magic," she sobbed. "Magic is just, just fooling. I know that. So I asked the Covenant to help me hide him."

Zanne's mother smiled at her ruefully, thinking how little

parents understand of how a child sees the world. In Garth valley the word "magic" was not used much. It was considered undignified to use the same word for Covenant work and for silly tricks. And yet the two were one.

"Not all magic is fooling, Zanne. Watch this."

She half-turned and stretched out one hand toward the setting sun. She brought the hand back and held it out, a closed fist. When she opened her fingers, in the cup of her palm there was a curl of deep glowing red. The warmth from it wrapped them both around. Zanne, who had been ice-cold and shivering with fright, felt the glow run through her.

"That is the sun, Zanne. The heat of the sun. I call it and it comes to me. If anyone's stove goes out in Garth valley, I go and light it again—straight from the sign and center of all fire on earth.... You know that. Don't you think that's magical?"

Zanne shook her head, confused. "But that's covener's work. That's real."

"It is real, and it is magic. And one day, Zanne, you will be a covener yourself."

Arles looked at the giant oak. The trunk was split again now. The tree would need some care if it was to live after that upheaval. She considered the power needed to meld a living human body into oak wood, considered what power like that might do to her valley, wielded by a playful ten-year-old child. She had been watching, waiting. She had hoped her talented little daughter might have a few more years of freedom. But the oak told her this couldn't be.

The little girl hiccuped, and knuckled her teary eyes.

"Oh, my baby," sighed Arles. "My poor little baby. I'm afraid it's time you went to school."

# CHAPTER 2

THERE WERE PENSIONER schools in every settlement and more organized institutions in most tradetowns. There was only one Covenant school. It was at Hillen in the north west. Around Hillen, as over the little hills and valleys of Zanne's part of Inland, there had been a city once. Now there was a bare, clean country of moors and marsh and clefts of oakwood. Settlements were few, and farmers tended great intakes of moorland instead of small, rich valleys. To reach this region out of Mid-Inland was a long journey, but rarely dangerous except in winter. The road to Hillen was well protected.

The tradestown that had grown up around the Covenant school was a crisscross of gray stone houses that appeared like a granite cairn in the distance as travelers approached across the moor. And in the center, like a stray shoulder of mountain jutting into the streets, was Hillen Mound.

Long ago in the years of change these mounds had been raised by the first coveners and their people; partly by magic and partly by hand tools. At that time, when the new Covenant with creation had just been made, it had seemed necessary for people to live *in* the earth. Once there were mounds everywhere. Most of them had fallen into disuse. There was one near Mosden that had had to be filled in because the roof had started to collapse. But Hillen remained: a labyrinth of halls and corridors, dormitories and studios, all buried under a canopy of stone and grass-grown soil.

It was the hidden heart of Inland, guarded by the thirteen Teacher-Coveners. Girls and young women with a talent for magic came here from all over the country, to become coveners or perhaps even teachers themselves. It was hard for a child of eleven or twelve years old to leave her friends and family, and the light and air; and all her freedom. It was hard too for her parents to give her up. But it was the same for any trade. The child must often leave home and grow up in someone else's house to learn the best of a skill. And everyone understood that the separation was necessary. Untrained power could not be left loose in the delicate web of magic that was Inland.

Zanne arrived at Hillen with her father at dusk on an early autumn day. She felt very small when they came to the doors of the school. Up close, the mound seemed enormous, looming over them and making the close gray streets look dark and strange.

A schoolgirl doorkeeper dressed in olive green took them to Tecov Elima, the present Holder of Hillen. Zanne sat beside her father, sleepy and bewildered, in a small room full of silvery lamplight. She only woke up when she realised Father was saying good-bye. And until that moment the journey had been an exciting adventure: saying good-bye to mother and Kila and Bren; the day's bumpy ride to Mosden and more good-byes to Grandma and Grandpa Weaver. Then seven more days by carrier—eating in strange inn common rooms, sleeping in strange beds, making friends with the wagoners and their oxen. Now suddenly she knew the truth, as she had known it the day Uncle Lol left and Mother looked at her with such pity and resolve. She grabbed Father's hand, tears springing in her eyes.

"Papa, don't leave me—" she wailed. "I'll be good, I promise. I'll never do magic again." She hadn't called him "papa" since she was a baby.

Hurst Weaver didn't get a chance to reply. That other figure, the stranger robed in midnight blue, swooped down on Zanne. Under her robe the Teacher-Covener wore a white tunic and leggings—the moon in a night sky. Her hair was brown, flashed and dashed with silver. It glittered in the lamplight as did her eyes, turned on Zanne like two compelling stars.

"Zanne," she said sternly, and not to a child. "You cannot keep that promise. Nor can you be allowed to live in the world until you have learned how to use the power that is in you. But if you choose I will take your talent away *now*. And then you can go home."

After a long moment Zanne said, "I'll stay."

She hugged her father.

"Be good," muttered Hurst, swallowing hard. "Your mother and I are proud of you."

Then Teacher-Covener Elima had mercy on them both, and sent him away to fetch Zanne's box and take it to her room. And Zanne wept her heart out, her head pillowed in her arms on the Holder's desk. Tecov Elima stood by without saying a word, until she touched the child's shoulder and said quietly:

"Enough."

There were a few girls—those with no close relatives or "changelings" born to people who had no magic in them—to whom coming to Hillen was coming home. Most shared Zanne's experience of shocked homesickness. But Zanne had more problems. She was a good year younger than any other pupil in the school. Worse than that, Zanne didn't know it, but a rumor had gone around the youngest students before she arrived that they were to be joined by a "child prodigy."

29

The doorkeeper took Zanne to her bedroom and left her there. The little girl saw a dimly lit space, and two other girls sitting cross-legged on mattresses on the floor. Her own box and bedding roll had been poked into the murkiest corner.

"Oh, I think you're in the wrong place," said Zanne politely. "This is my bedroom."

The two girls looked at each other and sniggered. One of them was plump, brown-haired and brown-eyed. The other was skinny with a crop of chestnut curls and very wide open, insolent blue eyes.

"Oo-arh," mimicked the blue-eyed one. "This is *moiy* bedroom!"

Zanne flushed but kept her temper. Mother had warned her that new girls are teased at school.

"Do we share? I'm sorry. I didn't know."

"She didn't know," cackled the plump brown one. "Well, well. She isn't as clever as she's supposed to be."

"She doesn't know *everything*!"

Zanne stood there, too bewildered by this unprovoked rudeness to defend herself, and someone else appeared out of the shadows—an older girl. She stood up from a little desk that Zanne had not noticed, by the fourth bed place.

"Agre!" she said sternly, frowning at the brown girl.

"Solin!"

The blueeyed one made a face.

"You ought to be ashamed of yourselves."

She turned to Zanne.

"You must be Zanne. Welcome. I'm Sinte, your room mother. Don't take any notice of these little midges ..."

Zanne's mouth dropped open. The girl's skin was *black*. Zanne had never seen anything so beautiful and strange.

"Why—what's wrong, child?"

30

"Is it magic?" gasped Zanne, "that makes you look like that?"

Agre and Solin hooted in delight.

"Oooh—baby's never been off the farm before!"

"Be quiet!" shouted Sinte. "Where are your manners? Don't mind them, Zanne. They're just nasty little creepy-crawlies."

Zanne's mouth was trembling but her head was high.

"I don't mind," she declared. "I'm a covener's daughter. I know how to behave."

"A covener's daughter!" shrieked Solin.

"Oh my!" crowed Agre. "Oh, what an *honor*!"

Now even Sinte was having to control her giggles. The spectacle of Zanne, so small and countrified and so full of injured pride, was almost too comical to resist.

"Out!" she snapped. "Get down to hall, you two. Zanne wants some peace to do her unpacking."

For that night and for the next day or two, Sinte firmly protected the newcomer, so that Agre and Solin had to accept a truce within the bedroom. And she taught Zanne kindly the ways of the school. But Sinte could not always be there. Zanne had to find her own way for the most part. She was abashed to discover that it was no special privilege to be a covener's daughter, to find people laughing at her slow country speech. She had her own olive green smocks and leggings, woven and cut and stitched by the best weaver in Inland. But people laughed at Father's homespun, and wore by preference "trade-goods" that Zanne quietly despised.

In Garth valley everyone was lightskinned, with eyes and hair in shades of brown. Townsend yellow heads were the height of human variety. Zanne was astonished to see black and brown and golden faces, showed her astonishment, and was struck down by horrible embarrassment. And stranger than that—there were people here who did not keep the

31

Covenant. There were girls who wore brooches and rings and had different clothes for every day of the week. Hillen diet was as restrained as anyone could desire, but there were girls who had rich and riotous food parcels from home. And nobody seemed to notice. The Teacher-Coveners did nothing. The little girl who had once envied a band of outlaws was scandalised. She knew people in towns behaved this way. But surely wicked excess should be forbidden at the Covenant school!

Covener training was divided into three stages: Inception, Continuance and Flores; about eight years of study. Most of these years were spent in the Mound. At some point in Continuance or Flores, each young woman as she felt ready would set off alone on her choice journey. The choice journey was used by all Inland, before any important task or change. It was a way of detaching the mind from its fixed paths, to make a major decision consciously instead of sliding into it on habit or other people's expectations. It was scarcely possible that a girl born magical would decide not to be a covener, but still the formal choice must be made. After this wandering time, which might last a year or more, a girl was called "covener", although her training might go on for quite a while.

Apart from the choice journey, older students came and went freely: some making long family visits, some studying year in, year out. Consequently there was a great difference in ages—from little girls to women who looked quite grown up to Zanne, all learning to be coveners.

In the autumn evenings the great hall where the students ate their meals was cleared of its trestle tables after supper. Almost all of Hillen gathered there—farmgirls, towngirls, girls from the sea coast, shy foresters who looked askance at such innocent luxuries as tables and chairs. Little "insects"—as the Inceptors were called—ran about, scuffled and chattered and yelled. Young women, coveners already and waiting to be placed, sat in groups sharing the Flores' meager allowance of thin ale. A few of them had babies. It was not uncommon for a marriage or a betrothal to be contracted in the later course of a Hillen career. There were usually visitors too: middle-aged and elderly women come to Hillen to consult the thirteen, or to rest and renew themselves.

The kitchen hatches were closed. On the long raised platform at the end of the hall stood thirteen chairs, lacquered in midnight blue. Each high back was decorated with the moon in a different phase. Here the Coven of Hillen would preside on ceremonial occasions, but now the chairs were empty. Over the platform, and over the noise and stir of the students, lay the silver and golden dusk of the Mound. Gnarled pillars like the roots of great living trees were sprinkled with firefly sparks, and the vaulted ceiling was spread with tiny lights like drifts of stars.

Zanne wandered alone up to the platform and perched on the edge of it miserably. She huddled her homespun jacket around her shoulders. The hall was adequately but not luxuriously heated by its one sunstove. She was thinking of Garth. There would be sweet chestnuts in the woods now, and hazel cobs. She thought of the autumn wind rushing across the downs, plunging through the valley and roaring in Garth beeches. There were gardens in the sunken crown of Hillen Mound. Every day Zanne was sent out with the rest of her Inception class to work for Tecov Etmel Gardener. She would gaze over the rim of the bowl, over the roofs of Hillen to grim beast-backs of dun moorland. She would not be going home for Midwinter, nor even for Spring Moon. Not until Summer came. She was trying to be brave, but it seemed very hard.

She had been at school a month now and it seemed like

forever. All the other Inception girls were as teasing and hostile as her roommates. The truth was some Teacher-Coveners were not quite wise in their treatment of the "new baby." Some of them remembered Arles of Garth at Hillen with particular affection and favored her daughter. Others were sorry for the little ten-year-old, torn away from home, and were overprotective. Zanne noticed nothing. She was used to loving attention; she had always been praised and admired. She only thought the other girls were very mean and nasty.

There were flashes down in the hall of colored fire, little birds conjured out of apple cores, a talking shoe that nobody would own to, walking around by itself and causing much hilarity. Zanne knew she could beat all of that. But no one had invited her to play, and she was too proud to ask. Anyway, since she had lost Uncle Lol, she had had no heart for illusion tricks.

A group of older Inceptors went by. They passed the new "insect" with condescending glances. Zanne observed a tall dark girl she had noticed before for her uncovenanted town clothes and uncovenanted long hair, done up always in a fanciful array of braids. That was Dimen Roadkeeper she had been told, the richest and the prettiest girl in Hillen. Zanne was disgusted that such "qualities" should be admired. Zanne glared.

She expected to be ignored. She was getting accustomed to that strange experience. She had almost forgotten the glare and was picking listlessly at the hem of her smock when suddenly someone was standing in front of her.

Dimen folded her arms, a curl of mischief in the corner of her pretty mouth.

"Well, what is it?" she demanded mockingly. "Have I spilled my dinner down my smock or what?"

Zanne was overcome with remorse. "Oh—I am sorry."

She blushed crimson. "Mother told me not to notice if people weren't fettled right. There's wickeder things than waste."

Dimen stared at the homespun insect: an absurd little figure, from her rough yellow head to her unshod horny feet. She began to laugh.

"What's so funny?" demanded Zanne, on her dignity.

"You," said Dimen candidly. And then, because she had a kind heart as well as a pretty face. "Us. The two of us. It beats me how Inland can hold us both."

She sat down on the platform. She knew Zanne's name; Hillen was not so large that newcomers could easily be missed. They discovered that they were neighbors. The Roadkeepers were of Mosden.

"You must know my grandma and grandpa!" cried Zanne.

Dimen laughed again. "Do you know how many people live in Mosden?"

"Too many," answered the little covenanter firmly. This time, they both laughed together.

Then Zanne sighed. "You know," she said. "I feel like a seed."

"A seed?"

"I lived in the air, on a stalk of wheat. And you were—er, on a flower. And all these others, all different too. But now we're all buried in the same earth. It's horrible, everything's gone dark, we can scarcely breathe. But we know we have to be here. This is where we have to start from. Do you think that's why they teach us under earth? I suppose the school could be in other places. . . ."

Dimen drew her feet up on the dais and wrapped her arms around her knees. She gazed at Zanne admiringly.

"I do like ideas," she drawled, only half teasing. "I never have them myself. I can't afford to be clever, you know. I'm too pretty—people wouldn't like it."

Dimen's little entourage did not see her again that evening. By the time they parted for the night the two strangely matched youngsters were friends, and would remain so, to the lasting astonishment of the Hillen community.

Zanne began to know her way around the windowless corridors that were lit by silvery lamps at night and mysterious filtered sunlight by day. She was absorbed into the routine of Inception. There were pensioner classes of writing, reading, and arithmetic just the same as at home. Zanne had no trouble with those. And she enjoyed working in the garden, except when distracted by homesickness.

But when it came to the other classes that began when she was settled in, Zanne was very puzzled. First thing every morning she and her group had to go to Tecov Josian to perform strange physical exercises. Zanne, tree climber, farmworker, was as supple and strong as most twelve-year-olds.

"But what is it all for?" she asked Josian. "And when am I going to start learning magic?"

"You have already begun," said Josian, who did not believe in burdening little girls with long lectures. They would learn in time about the link between body and mind, between one kind of effort and another. "This is magic," she stated flatly, pulling Zanne further into a painful stretch.

After that there was a class called "Inland," which could be about anything, Zanne found—about the street plan of a town or the insides of a flower or how to mend a lobster pot. Sometimes it was all stories about Inland's past, right back to the "land of the towers of light." Tecov Elima took this class herself. She seemed not to distinguish between the knowledge of a girl like Zanne, who had been familiar with her mother's books and papers, and another who had never learned to read. Zanne had always been quick to learn. She soon saw that the "Inland" class was not about how much you knew. It was about patterns—how one thing is like another. A tree is like a town. A river is like a cutting tool. . . . She was delighted. But when she announced her discovery, Tecov Elima—though she smiled—said no, that's not quite so. This lesson was "magic" too.

The third part of Hillen's magic teaching was the worst disappointment of all. A group of the youngest Inceptors sat in that filtered distant sunlight in a studio with pale wood-paneled walls. Tecov Coren was in charge. Zanne was excited. She knew that Coren (who also governed the kitchens) was the Shifter of Hillen: covener of the magic people called "world shifting." Now at last something must happen. Tecov Coren was stout and elderly, with red cheeks and sharp eyes. She handed out wooden puzzles, the kind of thing Garth children might be given at Spring Moon or on a birthday. Slip a piece into its right place—but every other piece moves with it. Start again, and find a way to carry the pattern along from one move to the next, never losing one part to gain another. Zanne finished her first puzzle long before anyone else. She showed it confidently to Tecov Coren: an angled ball brightly garlanded in painted flowers and leaves. The Tecov smiled a little, made two sharp moves with her knobbly, shiny-knuckled fingers and handed the toy back, totally jumbled once more.

"Now solve it again, while I watch."

Zanne could not. She had no idea how she had worked it out. Tecov Coren shook her head.

"That is not the lesson, Zanne. You have not understood the lesson at all. Step by step! That is the only way in magic."

It was lucky for Zanne that Dimen had decided to adopt her, otherwise her first seasons at Hillen would have been very miserable. And not only because of incomprehensible

lessons. Whenever a Teacher-Covener said, "Zanne, that's
well done. You're as bright as your mother!" her classmates
were seething. Whenever Tecov Josian let Zanne off the
hardest exercises in Link class, eyes were meeting bitterly
behind her back.

Zanne had been taught to speak of the Covenant as simply
and plainly as possible. This sounded like stupidity to many
of the girls, brought up in less strict communities. But being
stupid didn't help the prodigy, because her most ridiculous
remarks seemed to win totally unearned approval.

"Where is the Covenant?" asked Tecov Elima.

"It's in me," answered Zanne blithely, ignorant of the
proper answer, which was *The Covenant is in the mind and
heart of every individual who lives by free will in What Is and
with What Is. . . .*

"Correct, my child."

Elima flattened Zanne by adding in a menacing tone, "At
least let us hope so!" But the other Inceptors didn't notice
that. It infuriated them that Zanne showed no fear of the
Holder and would bounce up to her and chat as if Elima was
just another Garth farmer.

Her room-mates were waiting for her outside in the corridor with a girl called Epair, a tall, black-haired twelve-year-
old who had been the best at magic before Zanne came.

"You mustn't talk to Holder Elima like that," said Agre.

She looked to Zanne like a brown hen with a beady eye,
peck-peck-pecking with her mean sharp beak.

"You must get up and curtsey before you answer a
question," explained Solin, with a smirk.

Peck, peck, peck. A brown hen, a red one, and a black one.

"You're fooling. Nobody else does that."

"You don't show any respect for the Holder."

"I show her as much respect as I show myself," said Zanne
stoutly. "Under the Covenant, all people of Inland are equal."

"Oh, you little prig."

"Your head's as big as one of your mama's prize turnips."

"Tell us, Zanne. If you're so good at magic, why don't we ever see you prove it?"

Zanne didn't mean to do it, but she couldn't resist. Three prize hens stood in front of her. They caught sight of each other and squawked in outrage. Zanne walked away laughing. She hoped it would take hours for them to stop seeing each other like that.

Dimen, who had been waiting to meet Zanne after class, was watching from the end of the corridor. She shook her head sadly.

"You shouldn't have done it, Zanne."

"But they tease me so."

"Well, you do ask for it, my dear turniphead. You *are* a little prig."

But Zanne saw no fault in herself. And she wouldn't listen to Dimen. In spite of the difference in their ages, Zanne was well aware that her quick mind was usually ahead of the older girl's. Dimen never denied this, and so her criticism, always gently and mockingly given, lost its weight.

It was the dream-door that led to Zanne's downfall. Ironically, the Inceptors didn't even plan it that way.

Winter had set in and the Inception girls were prisoners in the Mound. There were no visits to the tradeshops, no moorland walks. Apart from a mild celebration of Midwinter, Hillen observed the season in retreat and quiet. When they were older, the coveners would remember with regret these few years in which they were able to share the moods of the earth so fully. There would not be much chance of winter sleep in the rest of their busy lives. But the first time it was hard. Especially after the snow had gone, and it seemed spring would never come. The bowl garden was dank and dismal. Rows of blue winter cabbages and curly kale kept mealtimes healthy but were not an inspiring prospect.

Zanne caught a bad cold. (Hillen magic did not protect the students from minor infections.) Tecov Coren was concerned, and prescribed hot malted milk at bedtimes—an unheard of luxury. By this time hardly any of the Inceptors would speak to Zanne, even to tease her.

So she was very wary when one night Agre and Solin cornered her in the bedroom. Agre watched the door while Solin came up to Zanne's corner, her blue eyes gleaming.

"What do you want?"

"D'you want to join in a magic game, Zanne?"

"What sort of a game?"

It was this. Agre and Solin, the liveliest of Inceptors, had decided to escape from the Mound. A girl called Instar, who had a cousin in Flores, had heard of something called "dream walking." It was book-magic, which was only studied in Flores. The bright sparks had approached Epair, the famous magic maker. But she was a cautious girl and refused to become involved. So they had to turn to Zanne. Curiously, although the child prodigy had shown little sign of her special talent, all her classmates believed in it.

"It's not breaking the rule," explained Solin plausibly, "because only our dreamselves will escape. And we do that in dreams all the time anyway."

Zanne was flattered. She would not have made the first move, but she was tired of being at war. She didn't take naturally to having enemies.

"All right, I'll try it. But how will you get the book?"

"Ssh!" hissed Agre from the door. "Sinte's coming."

Instar had already managed to sneak into the Flores library, pretending to be on an errand for her cousin. She was chased out. Some of those texts were dangerous for children even to be near. But she had the dream book. She managed to

40

pass it to Zanne the next day, when all the Inceptors were out in the gardens. Zanne stuffed it under her smock and smuggled it back indoors.

In the dark of Hillen, the under-earth dark that flowed back so swiftly whenever the displacing light retreated, Zanne lay on her small bed. She had been reading the book-magic by the light of a stub of candle, but now she'd put the candle out. She had never seen magic written down in words before. None of her mother's books were magical, not in this way. They were all about sheep, or vegetables. Or else just stories. She had a sneaking feeling mother would not approve. And yet it was exciting to feel how easily the knowledge came out of the words. Now that she had read the passages on dream walking, she knew she could do it.

For minutes she could see nothing. Then the granite walls began to sparkle faintly, borrowing brightness from the silver-lit corridor outside. In a little while she could make out three other mattresses, unrolled on the floor, and the hollowed shelf above each where the girls kept their few possessions. She could see Sinte's low desk and the square of rush matting beside it. Sinte was a Continuer and had earned some privileges. Zanne noticed that, just as the book had told her, she was not actually "seeing" these things. She saw only dim outlines. But if she let her mind play, it began to make up the rest. . . .

The bedroom door opened. Silver light flooded in. Sinte carrying a moonlamp, stood over Zanne's mattress.

"Why, young'un, you're in bed early. Are you feeling poorly?"

The black-skinned girl knelt down, looking concerned. A kind hand was laid on Zanne's brow. She felt a twinge of guilt.

"It's all right. I'm just tired."

Sinte frowned. She hoped Zanne wasn't getting ill again.

She had left the hall to study in peace before her insects came to bed. Instead she crept away, dowsing the moonlamp in her hands.

A few moments later Zanne sat up. Everything in the room was perfectly visible. She stood and looked down in pleased amazement at her own body lying peacefully asleep. Then she went out, down through the hill and past the Holder's study to the gloomy entrance hall. She lifted the latch on the small door set in one leaf of the big ones, and then she was outside the Mound.

It was a rainy evening in Hillen. Zanne in her nightsmock didn't feel the cold or wet. She had the freedom of the town. Even the cats couldn't see her. She went into an inn where tradesfolk were settling at long tables to eat pies and drink warmed ale. The little bean pies were served by the half-dozen, wrapped in a napkin in a wicker basket. Zanne took one and ate it; it was extremely good. The robbed diner made no outcry, for there were still six little pies in her napkin. Zanne laughed in delight, and no one heard her.

There was a flaw in the plan. It turned out that no one else could work the magic. The conspirators had hoped Zanne would be able to teach them, but she could not. Instar claimed she got a sickish feeling from looking at the words, but that was all. However, Zanne discovered that she could take people with her, one or two at a time. She needed only to think of a name and imagine a face: and that girl left her body behind and came out of the Mound too. At first it was only Instar, Agre, Solin, and Instar's special friend Gyptis. But the secret got out. Soon all the Inceptors were clamoring to join in. Zanne was taking girls out every night. The only person who resisted temptation was Epair. And everyone knew she was just sulking.

Tradesfolk made no complaints. The rule (so the Inceptors

42

told themselves) was not broken. Sinte observed gladly that her youngest charge had at last become popular.

Half a month after Zanne first began to dream, an attack of listless tiredness began to run through Inception. It was now Trime, the third moon. Soon winter's imprisonment would be over. Zanne would have liked to give up dream walking. But it was not so easy. There were girls who had not yet had a chance to go out, and she didn't want to seem ungenerous. Besides, she had come to Hillen to learn how to use her power—and nobody seemed to be teaching that in the lessons.

By the half moon of Trime, three of the girls who had adventured out with Zanne were lying in the little-used infirmary. And Hillen Coven knew, to its horror, that something terrible had somehow entered the granary of Inland. Thirteen minds united to search their own hearts, and then to sift, incredulously, the good seed corn. The Mound was closed, so no evil could escape. The whisper passed, shudderingly: there is a mind-eater among us. And an uglier, older name than that ... *vampire.*

The Tecovs did not yet announce their fear, hoping to deal with the infection without scandal. An atmosphere of troubled pervaded Hillen, but it was not enough to dissuade Zanne from leading a few more escapes. She had her suspicions about the girls in the infirmary. But Agre and Solin were all right. And she was only ten and she could dreamwalk every night without ill effects. She couldn't believe there was anything seriously wrong with those others.

On the twelfth night of Trime she lay on her bed while everyone else was in hall (except her two companions for the night, lying in their own rooms). She pictured the two girls who were coming with her, then let her mind play, dreaming with eyes open. But something hampered her. A face appeared in the strangely visible night room, as if painted on the darkness. A warm, freckle-dusted skin, a snub nose, hazel eyes, and a shock of tightly twisting light brown curls. Gyptis. It was easy to remember Gyp, with that hair. Zanne had had no trouble in taking her out. The face grew more and more distinct. It looked pale and wan—and suddenly horribly frightened. Zanne was frightened too. She tried to twist her head away, but the face only drew closer. She realized in shock that Gyptis could see her. The fear in the other girl's eyes grew. It was fear of Zanne! Closer and closer. . . The dream room turned over. Zanne was looking down, into the terror-stricken eyes. . . She screamed—and sat up with a jerk, her heart thumping, her palms sweating.

Teacher-Covener Elima was standing by her bed.

Zanne spent the rest of the night quarantined in an empty bedroom in Flores, in deep disgrace.

Six girls, Inceptors with receptive, vulnerable minds, had been in real danger. But the child was innocent. Holder Elima had proved that. She felt almost inclined to laugh to think of the horrors they had imagined, when the culprit was just this ignorant baby: a mouse stirring the cloak of evil.

However, Zanne was punished enough. The next day, Holder Elima asked some penetrating questions, and discovered the trick of "sending" that Zanne had learned from her uncle. There followed a severe lecture on the perils of mind magic.

"Dream walking is very exhausting, Zanne. But you are not exhausted. Do you know why? You stole the strength you needed, from those girls who had opened their minds to you. Just like a big bully stealing sweets. It is because of this danger that a covener will never, ever use the power of her mind on other individuals. That is forbidden. She will always work through What Is, and in What Is—through the natural world. You must remember that, my child."

That was a terrible half hour in the Holder's study. Zanne had seen the cool, kindly moon before. Now she met Night, Holder of Inland, and discovered there existed, after all, a proper distance between that presence and a vain, over confident apprentice.

In the Inceptors' magic class Tecov Coren had them all standing, admitting miserably, one by one, that they had been involved in the dream-escape. She berated them furiously on the evil and danger. Even the Hillen Coven feared to use this kind of power, so terribly close to wicked abuse, to mind destruction. . . .

"I—I didn't know it was wrong," sobbed Zanne. "It was so easy. Any—anybody could do it if they tried—"

Tecov Coren scowled at her, with the suspicion of a twinkle in her sharp eyes.

"Oh, Arles was right to send you to us. Young as you are, young as you are. A great lumbering bullock with the mind of a gnat—that's you, Zanne of Garth."

The vision Zanne saw had been provided by Holder Elima. The actual sufferers knew nothing. When they learned that Zanne had been draining them to fuel the escapes they might have been scared of her. But she was in so much trouble they had to sympathize instead. At least, after this, the new girl could no longer be resented as a priggish teacher's pet.

Zanne apologized to everyone, including Sinte, whose trust she had abused. She wrote to her mother and received a reply that she kept for years. For nearly a half month she was unnaturally subdued. But then Spring Moon came, with painted eggs and new clothes, and the trouble was behind her.

And after Spring Moon, there came another change. One day Tecov Coren distributed smooth pebbles instead of wooden puzzles.

"Now," she began. "Who can tell me what the Link is?"

"It's our exercises, Tecov."

"And—?"

Even Zanne was silent for once.

Coren smiled. She had been teaching little Inceptors for fifty years. She still loved this moment.

"The Link is this. It is the power we use in all world-shifting magic. By the laws of this world of ours effort is effort, achievement is achievement, whether in the body, or the mind, or in magic. The physical exercises you have learned have had one purpose, to teach you what it means to put your whole self into something you want to do."

"Now I want you to lift these pebbles from the floor. Not in illusion but in world-shifting truth. Think of this room as a pattern. You know about patterns now, and how much care you must take to change one without losing it. Now push. Push the world. Put your *backs* into it!"

There was a moment's concentrated silence. And then a concerted gasp of delight. A class full of Inceptors, sitting cross-legged with folded hands. A class full of little pebbles floating in the air.

None of the others had put an uncle into an oak tree, but most had had similar accidents on a smaller scale. This was different and they all knew it. They were in control. They knew how to do it again.

Of course it was Zanne who wanted to know why. Anyone could pick up a pebble. There was no need for magic.

"Yes, you can move a pebble, Zanne, but can you move a mountain?"

"No, but—"

"Then have patience, child. Step by step, from the pebble we will reach the mountain."

"But Tecov, long ago in the land of the towers of light—couldn't people move mountains without magic?"

46

The class giggled. Most of them didn't believe in those old stories at all.

Tecov Coren only answered firmly.

"Perhaps. But we don't have such power now. We have only the Covenant, so you had better learn to use it."

In New Summer when it was Zanne's birthday, Dimen gave her a pin, a little circle of silver set with freshwater pearls. It was too much, of course; no member of Garth meeting would have been seen dead wearing such a thing. But Zanne wore it, out of loyalty.

Some people assumed that worldly Dimen tolerated the little farm girl out of kindness. Others were disappointed that a good covenanter had been led astray. But the Road keepers had no magic. All her life Dimen had been a "changeling"—and then at Hillen she had found her town ways and looks were equally out of place. She played up to the rôle expected of her; she had her pride. But there was another Dimen, serious and a dreamer, who had been very lonely until Zanne came along. As for Zanne, she did not see Dimen's wealth at all, except as a disadvantage which a good-mannered person ought to ignore. All she saw was her friend. And while the dream-door trouble made little lasting impact on her sunny and buoyant nature, this she would remember. It was the "uncovenanted" town girl who first showed her kindness, when she was new to Hillen, and everything was strange.

# CHAPTER 3

ZANNE LIVED AND worked five years at the Covenant school. She grew taller, but not very tall, and her yellow hair grew, if anything, yellower as if determined not to be outfaced by the dusk under Hillen Mound. She was free after her first year to return to Garth whenever she pleased. But she contented herself with one short visit a year and learned not to long for the valley. She felt it was wrong, under the Covenant, to be always rushing to and fro. There were many students who would never see their homes and families until they were coveners.

Lifting a pebble without touching it was delightful, but it didn't seem to have much to do with Covenant work. Later the Inceptors began to learn other kinds of world shift.

"To change one thing into another, or one world into another," said Tecov Coren, "you must find, at whatever depth, a unity between them. So you will hear stories of the Covener of Kor, who laid a knife on the ground and it became a river. River cuts earth. You won't be asked to do anything like that. But don't worry. You will find enough work in shifting Mid-Inland chalk mire toward good fertile soil."

Year by year, her knowledge and understanding grew. And it seemed to Zanne that she was learning at Hillen things that Garth and her mother had been telling her all her life: only she had been an unfocused child unable to see what was right in front of her.

She began to understand the magic of Inland—unseen and patient, working in the night of the mind like roots in the earth. The most ordinary commonplace things, like the sun in her mother's kitchen stove, revealed themselves as strange and marvelous. She knew now that the sheep didn't come down happily to shed their wool at the fleece harvest just because it was so. Generations of shifting by Inland's coveners had changed the world to this new pattern. It was magic too that kept Garth's small dairy herd in milk, although the cows were by no means always suckling calves. The apple orchards, the fields of wheat and beans, the humble potatoes, were tended by magic as well as by human hands. Even the weather was tempered, so Inland rarely had to endure a wet and rotten summer or a killing long frost.

At first, like many less thoughtful Inlanders, Zanne wondered why the covens didn't make life completely perfect. She had to give up that kind of complaint as she used more magic herself and came to grasp the size and complexity of the task. A covener did not work alone either. Every member of her meeting was part of her shifts and holdings. That gave her great strength, but it was something Zanne could hardly bear to think of. So many minds! Each of them able to affect your magic, accepting or refusing it. And beyond your own holding, there would be other settlements with needs to be parleyed and balanced. It was like the spiderweb the young men would make in their maypole dancing. And in the center of the web (though that center was always shifting) was Hillen Coven.

But so far Zanne didn't have to worry about such complications. At fourteen going on fifteen she was a Continuer. She could move pebbles, and more than pebbles. She could lift her own body twice her height into the air—but these and many other feats were confined to Tecov Coren's studio, sheltered and contained by the Hillen earth.

Zanne's formidable talent rarely showed itself in these years. She was a good pupil, willing and popular and hard-working: but her teachers kept her firmly to Hillen's routine exercises. There were no more adventures like the dream-door. Yet she learned something of the magic that Hillen called "forbidden"—the magic of the mind—and understood better how close she had come to horrible abuse of power in that escapade.

And if Zanne still felt sometimes that this tending of crops and helping of tradesfolks was a little flat and dull beside the old tricks Uncle Lol used to play, she never rebelled. She comforted herself with daydreams about the old "land of the towers of light" and went into the tradeshops of Hillen, admiring all the interesting tools that went up and down and round and round. . . . In Continuer patterning lessons, Tecov Pompe—a rather narrow woman—got very annoyed when Zanne started talking about how to "improve" a flour mill. Zanne didn't really know why, but she learned to keep such ideas to herself.

Hillen Coven watched the young Continuer carefully. She was much loved—in spite of her gifts—by the other girls. She played with the little Inceptors and talked seriously with Flores and with Hillen's learned visitors. She showed maturity as well as talent. She might be more than a covener. She might one day be a teacher herself.

Only one person spoke against Zanne, when the thirteen were discussing her future. That was Coren, the crabbed old Shifter. Coren loved the yellow-headed brat. Wasn't she the one who nursed the baby with malted milk and honey gruel when she was ill with homesickness in her first winter?

"Yet I have to say this," declared Coren grimly. "She is a child of Day. Everything comes easily to her, and what is easy is not magical. I am sorry, but I cannot foresee the shift that will bring her into Hillen Coven. I do not see her here." It was the Shifter's rôle to oppose the majority, and Coren was old and naturally contrary. Still she could not be overruled. The decision was set aside for another while.

Zanne knew nothing of this process. She only knew that after she was made covener, maybe she might be sent to the college at Kor to learn to be a teacher. Once she would have been frightened at the prospect of a life underground at Hillen. Now she was proud to think she might be chosen. Perhaps if she was a Tecov she would finally lose this feeling of restlessness.

In New Summer, just in time for her fifteenth birthday, Zanne came home to Garth. Dimen of Mosden came with her. Dimen was not so conscientious as Zanne. She often spent months at home, when her family called her. And so, by slipping and sliding, she had arrived at the same level as her friend, although she was nearly seventeen and might have been in Flores. No one at Hillen was concerned about this. The Teacher-Coveners, curiously enough, had great confidence in Dimen. In her own time, in her own style, she would make a wise and tolerant covener.

Dimen's clothes and manners had not changed. She caused quite a sensation when she stepped down from the ox wagon outside Garth Inn, and met the people who were waiting to collect goods from the carrier. But to Zanne's relief everyone was polite. Things went well at Townsend too. Father's present apprentice, a boy called Fela, was instantly smitten. Bren was impressed, and Mother and Father were just themselves. Zanne spent half an hour watching them all nervously. Would Dimen sneer at the country kitchen supper? Would Arles comment on that

51

uncovenanted jewelry and those extravagant braids? Then she relaxed, feeling ashamed of herself for her mistrust.

Dimen was given a room above the old dairy. The walls were bare and white, the uneven boards that had never been waxed or varnished were smooth as silk under her feet. On her hard, narrow bed was a coverlet woven in shades of green by the hand and eye of an artist. She looked out of an unglazed window at New Summer nightfall, a glow like honey still lying in the west, and not one light else but the moon and stars. A little guiltily, she dowsed her own trade-bought moonlamp, stretched her arms wide in the dark, and laughed.

The day after Zanne's birthday, she and Dimen walked up to the first crest of the downs to see if Garth's flocks were moving yet. Zanne had intended a longer expedition, but Dimen refused. She said she had come to the country for a rest, not to go mountain climbing. So they spent a peaceful afternoon up on the smooth green shoulder above Townsend and Upper Valley farms, strolling between the gorse bushes. Larks sang loudly overhead; the "doeys" jumped and stared and scampered from underfoot. Dimen laughed at the doeys. It was the local word for a rabbit. For years she had heard Zanne use it and thought it meant a kind of dough-cake.

"Cakes don't hop around under the bushes," laughed Zanne. "Not even in the wilds of Garth."

"They might. If the covener had a silly sense of humor."

They settled on the turf at last, like the blue butterflies spreading their wings to the sun, and talked a little and dreamed in silence, in equal comfort. The light, dry, airy warmth was so different from Hillen. Heat up on the moor was a heavy thing, slow and low-lying as the heather.

Dimen showed Zanne a picture that she carried in her wallet. It was a magical toy: a square of fine linen that woke at Dimen's touch with the head and shoulders of a young man, in living depth and detail. His eyes looked out ruefully, as if he didn't quite like the idea of being carried around in someone's pocket.

In Mosden there was not one covener but several. Each had her assistants, and they would trade magic; making pretty trifles like this for the townspeople. Zanne took the picture carefully, hoping her disapproval wouldn't spoil it.

"That's my Eko. His people are friends of my family, of course."

"And will you marry him?"

"I certainly will," said Dimen, smiling. She spoke lightly. But the look in her eyes told a different story.

"Won't you even have a baby first?"

Dimen threw back her head and laughed.

"Oh, Zanne! That's not the way we do things in town."

Zanne gave Eko back and saw him fade and be tucked away. She hoped she would be friends with him in time, but she knew Dimen wouldn't marry anyone for a few years yet and was glad of that.

Where would Zanne be in a few more years? She drew her knees up, leaned her chin on her folded arms. It was haymaking weather, fleece harvest weather. Tomorrow what Bren called "Zanne's rest cure" would be over. She would be set to work again, as always when she came home. That was what she wanted, to work hard in the hot sun, pick up sheep ticks and get grass seeds under the skin of her palms. She wanted to be Zanne Townsend again. At Hillen she was Zanne of Garth. The Inland way was that you were known by the name of your farm or by your parents' trade, until you did something different or moved away. It wasn't important. Still, it sometimes gave Zanne a strange, cold feeling to know Bren would be "Bren Townsend" all his life. He would never leave this valley, except for a few trips to

Mosden. Everyone around him would know him and he would know everyone, as well as he knew his own fields. Not that she couldn't share the farm if she wanted to. But it wouldn't do. That wasn't what she wanted. The problem was, she couldn't think what she did want. To be a covener in another valley like this one? Or to be a teacher? It troubled her that she could not be sure, even though the choice was still years away.

Yesterday, on her birthday, she had been in the kitchen with Arles in the late afternoon. She and her mother sat on the kitchen doorstep with their feet out in the sunny yard, talking about Zanne's future. There was a bowl of yellow rose-apples between them—so called because they ripened early in the year when the wild roses were in bloom. Zanne picked up an apple and held it cupped in her hand. It was so round and sure, it made her fingers glow.

"I don't care what I do," she said. "So long as I have a life that's whole. That I can hold in my hand like an apple—do you see?"

Mother shook her head, with a knowing air.

"You will never do that."

Mother could be irritating sometimes. Returning to the present, Zanne looked at Dimen, who seemed to have fallen asleep. It was good to know that at least one thing was settled. Whatever happened they would still be friends. When we are old, she thought, we'll talk sometimes of the time she came to the country, and found that Garth dough-cakes have long ears and cotton-tails. And no shadow crossed the sun. Nothing in Zanne whispered to her of any other future.

Dimen opened her eyes.

"Thinking secrets?"

"No—I was just thinking I'm glad I'm only fifteen."

"That's not polite," said Dimen, grinning. "Well, help me

up. This old lady is getting hungry."

They went down from the hill by Upper Valley. As they passed the farmyard Mir was there, leaning on the gate with his brother Kest.

"Seen the sheep?" he called.

The sons of Upper Valley had changed a good deal since Zanne Townsend went away to school. She was always puzzled when she met the friends of her childhood. Her visits were so short, it seemed as if only a few months had passed in Garth for her five years away. She knew that *she* was older but she couldn't imagine where these great creatures had come from—tall young women and youths with downy, sprouting beards. Mir, whom she had once decided to marry, and Kest, the elder brother, were now stalwart flores with broad brown shoulders and high-colored open faces.

"We've not seen them," called Zanne. "Didn' go so far enough."

She was glad she could still slip into country speech when she wanted to. It made her feel less of a stranger.

"Commen' up this evenin then? We're off to spy them, mebbe catch a fleece or two."

So Dimen and Zanne went over to the gate. They didn't want to go out on the downs again—Dimen had had enough strenuous activity—but they stayed to chat. The boys preened themselves on being introduced to Dimen. They teased her shyly for wearing shoes in summer. No wonder her feet were sore!

Now it had not crossed Zanne's mind that Mir might still recall that she had once proposed marriage to him, when she was ten and he was eleven years old. She conveniently used to forget Kest then because she had never liked him. But the Upper Valley boys did remember. To both of them it seemed that Zanne Townsend must be looking for a husband, if not now then one day soon. And Upper Valley was a good farm but they didn't care to share it. It would be a fine thing for one of them to marry a covener and get the chance to set up in another valley. A meeting always did an incoming covener proud with house and land. In half friendly rivalry, the brothers were out to make an impression.

Dimen saw this at once. She had been told about Mir, Zanne's childhood sweetheart. She also knew that Zanne had no idea what was passing through the young lads' minds. But there seemed little harm in it, so she let things go on, in banter and genial country sarcasm.

Mir and Kest wanted to see some magic. Illusion was a vice that Hillen students soon grew out of. They learned to see it as a misuse of power. But tricks were innocent enough if only meant in play. Zanne gave them a wisp of straw turned into a bunch of roses. Dimen took advantage of the barnyard cat, who had come stalking over to inspect the visitors. It turned green and made a short but boastful speech (in a Garth accent) on its prowess as a ratter.

The cat recovered and sat down suddenly, glaring at the four of them. It did not see the joke.

"Nawp," drawled Kest (the Garth way of saying "not good enough"). "We want some true magic."

Zanne was doubtful. Continuers were not supposed to attempt shifts and holds outside the Mound. But in the end she took a pebble and made it dance in the air. Dimen did the same; it was a little ballet. With a slow grin, Kest sought and picked up three stones as big as apples. He began to juggle neatly.

"That's good, eh," remarked Mir with simple pride. "He didn't go to school to learn that either."

"Taught myself," explained Kest modestly.

Then the contest began. It soon degenerated into a weight-lifting competition, brawn against magic. Dimen dropped out, laughing: Mir was never involved. It was Kest against Zanne—and of course she could not win on the terms dictated. The Link allowed her to move things without touching them. But she was on her own, without meeting or coven; her strength, however translated, was that of a small though sturdy fifteen-year-old girl. She knew this, but she was trapped. She was too young to know how to walk away from a fight and still keep her pride.

So in the end Kest bent to the massive stone mounting block that stood in the middle of the yard. Sweat broke out on his forehead, his face turned red as a beet under his tan, and the muscles across his neck and shoulders seemed about to burst through his skin. He lifted the block just far enough so you could see light between it and the ground.

Zanne didn't even try. She wished Tecov Zair was here, the Link teacher of Continuance. Tecov Zair would have shown this lout a thing or two. But even in her temper, she could see there was no point in telling Kest that.

The young man wiped his face. "My father could do 'ut," he declared breathlessly. "When he was my age. I never tried that before, myself."

He grinned at Zanne, large and glistening and unbearably pleased with himself.

"You show me, girl. Show me one thing you can do with magic that I can't do with my hands."

There was malice in his voice, under the honest boasting. Dimen heard it. She took a step toward Zanne, put a hand on her arm. But Zanne heard that note too, and instantly lost the remains of her self-command. Her gray eyes flashed a glance that hit Kest like a blow, full in the face. The big youth recoiled. Zanne had a sensation like pushing a closed door. The door opened at once. She knew outrage, not her own. Her victim was aware that someone was inside him. But there was nothing he could do. She had a vision, a strange vision of

57

silver, glittering creatures. He was struggling, panic stricken, to hide his secrets. But he could not hide. . . .

Then she was standing in the farmyard again. She felt a little sick, and not at all triumphant. Kest had paled visibly. Now dark color slowly rose again under his skin in a painful, ugly blush. He turned away, and almost stumbled into the farmhouse.

Mir looked from one girl to the other.

"Only a bit of fun," he muttered. "I'd better go see—"

He hurried after his brother.

It was just an awkward moment, a foolish end to a foolish quarrel. A hen came tripping around the end of the barn, clucking importantly.

"Come on. Let's go home." Dimen took Zanne's arm. "I know what you did," she told her, as she led the unprotesting girl away.

Zanne nodded dumbly.

"I saw—"

"You mustn't tell me. You must never tell anyone. You know that."

She had looked into Kest's mind, uninvited. This was forbidden territory. It should also have been far beyond her capacity. But at Hillen people had given up making pronouncements about Zanne's abilities.

The young magician seemed stunned, as well she might be. Dimen reassured her. She had seen Kest's eyes before he ran away. He was himself, uninjured. They went up through Townsend orchard, under the young apples and pears just setting in the gray-green leaves, and stopped by Arles' prized cluster of orange trees.

"Let me give you some advice," said Dimen firmly. "If you're sure you didn't hurt him—"

Zanne winced. "I didn't," she muttered. "I just looked—"

"Don't tell me 'it was easy'—or I will *smack* you. Well then, don't tell your mother. I know you're ashamed and you want to confess. But you'll just have to bite on that. Think of Kest. He knows what happened to him. And I'm sure he doesn't want anyone else to know."

Zanne gave her friend a scared, startled glance.

"You're right," she answered. "He doesn't."

They went indoors. Soon Zanne was behaving quite normally and cheerfully. Dimen was certain she had done right. Nothing had happened—simply a stupid piece of bad temper. It was best forgotten as soon as possible.

# CHAPTER 4

THE FLEECE HARVEST began. Its holiday mood filled the valley. The big fleece-stripping enclosure was raised on the green in front of the inn. The animals came each to their own yard and were brought down, jostling and noisy and excited as the children who ran with them. Everyone wore as few clothes as possible; hot, tanned skins exuded the strong greasy smell of the fleeces; and sheep ticks were a menace. The disruption and the fun would go on for days.

Once the fleeces were washed and baled, and the green cleaned of every scrap of wool, the sheep did not return to the downs at once. They had to be bathed until they smelled like roses, they had to stay in Garth as free and wicked as three-year-old children. In this way the magical bond between the people and their animals was maintained, and the covener and meeting learned of any threatening illness or trouble in the flock. There was always good food and plenty of beer at the fleece harvest. But no meat. It would not have appealed to anyone.

On the first day of stripping, the young men danced morris and maypole on the green outside Garth Inn. Covener Arles stood up on a barrel under hoops of fresh plucked roses and made a speech.

"The pride of Inland," she declared, "is in the strength and beauty of our fine boys—" A cunning deadfall arranged in the rose arbor at this moment gave way. The covener fell off her barrel laughing, doused in ale.

Zanne left Dimen with the merry crowd. She would not be lonely. She was already making friends. At this holiday, flores from vales around banded together "following the fleece." It was a time to make friends, to find sweethearts, a joyful escape from the isolating and sometimes weary round of life on an Inland farm. Zanne could be sure that she was free for hours. She had noticed, quietly, that Kest of Upper Valley was not among the harvest dancers.

She walked to the Moss, where a spur from the wagon road crossed it on a stout little stone built bridge. No one was watching her. It was strange how quickly the music and general ruckus faded away.

*Neah!*

Zanne jumped guiltily. A head with a cockeyed wreath of buttercups poked up over the wall of a pension garden. The sheep fleered at her with its intelligent yellow eyes, its long jaw working sideways.

"Ssh!" whispered Zanne, and laughed. "Don't tell."

The sheep laughed, "Nyah," leapt neatly over the wall and trotted away munching on a bunch of clove-scented carnations.

Then all was quiet. Zanne slipped down beside the bridge and began to make her way upstream. She was in shadow now, under arching hazels. The Moss ran loud and sweet, clear and dark, with crystal white bubbles around its rocks. She rolled her leggings above the knee and waded from pool to pool along the water margin, the sun striking in hot dapples on her shoulders where it came through the leaves. She had not walked like this, in the stream, since she was ten years old. She was following a trail—unseen, known only by magic; so her feet knew better than her eyes where she was going. Those she was following walked in the water

61

because they knew, as everyone knows, that the inconstancy of water protects, conceals. They didn't want the covener to be aware of them when they came this way.

She emerged from the hazel tunnel into a place where the stream spread itself more widely, with beaches of flint pebbles on either side. Above the beach on the Garth side were miniature cliffs. On the Mosden side, woods began: undergrowth tangling down over the stones and big trees looming at once behind. The air was full of honeysuckle sweetness, and a murmur of bees mixed with the chuckling of the water. Zanne walked for a while, following the invisible trail. Then the sound of the water grew louder and she saw ahead of her a place she had looked at in Kest's mind. The bank on her left-hand side, which was now about three times her height, was interrupted by a mass of fallen ruin stones. The blocks had pushed and tumbled over each other, dividing the Moss. The main stream flowed on, beyond a bar: but a part of it was forced to make itself a passage by jumping over stone. A thick, glassy rope of water plunged down into a bubbling pool.

Zanne stood frowning. She could remember this spot. It seemed much smaller than it had been when she was a little girl. In those days the pool was big enough for swimming. It was hardly more than a deep bathtub now. It puzzled her that she couldn't recall ever having explored those stones. She could see from here enticing triangles and slits of darkness; you wouldn't have thought any child could resist the promise of caves. Perhaps it was dangerous, and they had all been told to keep away. But she couldn't remember that either.

She began to climb. When she came to the entrance she regretted her smock, which she had left behind her. She was only wearing a singlet, it looked as if she would have to scrape all the skin off her arms to wriggle through. Then she remembered that Kest had to be able to get in here, and discovered that by sliding down under the first space, she found her feet in the opening of a fairly wide tunnel. At first it was formed by the blocks leaning against one another. Yellow claws of sunlight scratched their way in. A little farther on, she was really underground. She took a moon lamp from her pocket. It was a pebble she had picked up on Hillen moor. It was bound to her by affection now, as even the simplest object can be. Tecov Coren said light is in everything, there's plenty to go around. A little light—a *little* light—is the easiest kind of magic.

Holding the stone, surrounded by its mild silver glow, she walked on. There was a prickling at the back of her neck, goose pimples down her arms, that had nothing to do with cold or fear. She came to a regular shaped opening. It was a doorway. The original door had vanished long ago. The space had been blocked with earth and rubble and shards of rusty metal. But someone had made a way in, quite recently. She stepped through the hole.

They were waiting for her—Kest and an old man. They stood facing the door with their backs to the secret treasure. They must have heard her footsteps. Kest's face was bitter and angry.

"I knew you would come," he said.

The room was large, low and square. The ceiling and walls had been paneled in some dull, hard material Zanne could not identify; but the paneling was falling down, revealing bare stone. The lighting was by candles and two oil lamps. In Garth they didn't use magic light for ordinary domestic purposes; it had the disadvantage that it would fade if some part of a covener's attention was not always on it. Fuel was used sparingly, like any other resource. Kest must have been rifling Upper Valley's winter stores. Piles of rubbish lay about and lurked in the corners. But the treasures themselves

63

had been cleared of debris. There were ten of them, each about the size of a year-old heifer. They shone brightly: ten creatures of gleaming metal, so exactly angled and curved they could only have been tooled by unalloyed magic, not by human hands. Zanne's mouth dropped open.

"They're beautiful," she whispered at last.

Kest and the old man looked at each other warily. The oldster suddenly grinned, revealing a few crooked yellow teeth.

"There y'are," he exclaimed triumphantly. "Told 'ee there was no need to fret. I sees these things. I knows—"

He shambled forward, wiping a hand on the seat of his murky leggings and thrusting it at Zanne.

"It's young girl Townsend, ain't it? I thought 'ee meant t'other one. I thought 'ee meant the darkie lass."

Zanne knew him. He didn't belong to Garth. He was one of the pensioners of Clapperbridge, a settlement five vales or so up the Moss. He was weak in the head and a wanderer, had been that way for years. She remembered him from when she was a little girl: an odd shuffling figure, not very clean. He sometimes came to Townsend for a meal as he might to any farm. Bren always hated him. It was his duty to sit by the guest and serve him at table—and he did smell rather strong.

"It's Sear of Clappers," She greeted him kindly, letting him grasp her hand. "How are you, grandfather?"

"Oh, tolerable, tolerable."

She let the old man lead her around the lovely metal beasts.

"Ah fettled them," he explained proudly. "They were in a poor way when I found 'un. But Ah petted them and made them fearless."

He nodded and winked and made caressing gestures with his horny fingers. The beasts seemed to know him and gleamed brighter under his touch, and Zanne remembered that old Sear had a little magic in him. People hired him for it sometimes, the way a covener's assistant might be hired in town. But they also said (ungratefully) it was his uncovenanted magic that had made the man weak and silly.

"What are they, Sear?"

"Why, makers o' course. Like in the olden days."

Sear grinned.

"Ah found 'un. Ah cum 'ere years agone. Ah dig like a mouldlywarp acos Ah could smell 'un. Met-al. That smells strong. Ah tell all the folks but they don't pay no mind to me."

Kest was listening with folded arms.

"He's told everyone in three valleys," he remarked. "The old crazy. It's no account, because no one listens. But I followed him."

"And we dug the met-al beasts out, and we fettled 'em wi' sand and water. That wor a long job. Got to keep it a secret, see. Garth folk don't like the makers."

Zanne stepped around, staring with awe at the great shining beasts. She had never seen so much metal in one place. This was the vision that she had seen in Kest's mind.

"The room must have been airtight," she murmured. "Or they would have fallen into rust. Do you know what 'makers' are, Sear? They are tools. I've learned about them at Hillen. Tools that move on their own, and do the work of a hundred hands."

Sear nodded excitedly. He led her to a pile of small objects. He held one out to her: a little flat metal ring, burnished like a well-used knife blade.

"And these is what they makes!"

They weren't finger rings, or part of any tackle or harness she could think of.

"But what for?"

Sear's face fell. His mouth mumbled; he didn't have an answer. Kest was still hanging back sulkily.

"Just like a woman," he exclaimed bitterly. "*What's it for?* You're going to tell your mother, aren't you, Zanne Townsend? Bring the whole meeting down on us."

She didn't know herself what she had meant to do. She had followed the trail that she had plucked from behind Kest's eyes, almost as if sleepwalking. Now she saw in front of her an incredible treasure. All her life she had loved stories of the lost past. And here it was, shining and real. These giant tools must have been buried here since the towers of light stood over Garth valley.

"You're right," she agreed. "The meeting would only laugh."

Garth would call the makers a useless frivolity, she thought. In a community where every candle was counted, Kest must have put a lot of effort into sneaking out his supplies. She looked at a wooden bucket standing by the foot of one of the makers, a battered old wreck probably only held together by Sear's bit of magic.

"They'd call this wicked waste."

Kest nodded, watching her narrowly. Zanne understood that her mother and the meeting would not approve. But she had been away to school, and anyway had been brought up in a house where the "lost past" was viewed rationally, not as a horror. Kest knew that the people of Garth would do more than laugh if they knew about this "treasure." But he wasn't going to explain that to Zanne.

"Are you going to tell on us?" he asked.

"I can't tell," she declared. She wanted to win him over and persuade him she could be trusted. "We're not supposed to read minds. I'd be in trouble myself. I don't want to anyway. I want to share this. Will you let me come again?"

Kest grinned slowly.

66

"Told 'ee! Told 'ee!" crowed Sear. "She'm safe enough."

The three shook hands. It was like joining a children's gang, thought Zanne. And thereafter the gang met as often as they could, to play their exciting secret game.

Dimen went back to Mosden before the fleece harvest was over. She was a little surprised about the times that Zanne disappeared. It was only a short visit and her first to Townsend; she would have expected to see more of her friend. However, she had her suspicions, which were both right and wrong, about that handsome though irritating young man from the neighboring farm. It wouldn't be the first courtship to start with a quarrel. So Dimen made no comment, and took care no one at Townsend noticed Zanne's absences either.

The holiday should have been over for both of them soon after that. Zanne was to ride into Mosden with the local carrier: then she and Dimen would travel together the long wagon road to Hillen. But there was an unexpected delay. A bridge on the route from Mosden had been weakened by heavy weather earlier in the year. It was dangerous—the Midsummer train had to be canceled. Such accidents were a part of Inland life because roads were few and easy travel a luxury; not one of the first concerns of the Covenant. Zanne was not at all dismayed. She was very happy to be a farm girl for a while longer. And when the pleasant work in fields and yards was done, she had the makers to occupy her.

The old man took to Zanne at once. Kest was more wary. But when she came back a second time, without her mother or a pack of sniggering girls, he began to trust her. There was no more treasure. The only exit from the makers' cave was blocked solid with rubble. But the ten wonderful creatures were quite enough to absorb and fascinate three enthusiasts.

They were not all made on the same pattern. Zanne was fascinated to trace, in these giant forms, the simple hand tools that she knew well: a lathe, a spindle, a bit-and-brace drill, the screw of a cider press.

Just to polish the makers and play with them would have been enough for Sear. But Kest had bullied him into a further achievement, which was revealed to Zanne at the end of her second visit. The old man looked to Kest anxiously. Kest nodded. Sear drew himself up.

"Ah can magic them alive," he declared proudly.

He closed his eyes, screwed up his fists. Zanne held her breath, hardly able to believe it was possible. But it was so. Slowly, haltingly, the great metal beasts stirred. They raised their arms to each other in a ponderous dance. The spindles turned, the sliding heads began to move, the great glistening screw lifted from its bed. For a moment the dusky room was filled with lovely shining motion, and a clear chord of the sounds of metal on metal, echoing down the years from the lost past. Only for a moment. The old man let out his breath with a grunt and sat down abruptly on the floor, mopping his brow.

"Eh—Ah've done that thrice now. Eh—Ah'm getting good at that, Ah am."

The makers were dead again.

Kest scowled. He could see by the expression on Zanne's face that she was not very impressed.

"I suppose you could do better," he growled.

Zanne had been frowning, staring at him without seeing him. Suddenly she smiled.

"I think I could!" she cried. "I really think I could."

So began the most exciting magic Zanne had ever attempted. Just a few days ago she had been unwilling to lift a pebble because of Hillen's rule. She forgot that now. Besides, the makers in their underground den seemed so different from Garth's yards and fields; it was easy to imagine the one could not affect the other.

At first just the entrancing motion was enough. But Kest soon got tired of that. He was now convinced that Zanne had "let" him win their contest in the farmyard, to tease him: and she could really do whatever she pleased with the world. In his total ignorance of magic, he goaded Zanne on to do the impossible.

The makers were supposed to make things out of metal. Kest wanted to see them do it. Zanne pointed out they had no material. There was no such thing as spare metal in Garth. It was Kest who thought that the little silvery rings could be melded and worked over again. He teased and goaded Zanne into using her magic to shift a handful of the rings into a solid stick. The shift was not a good one. Inlanders did not use magic to work metal. The heart of a forge or smelt house would be sunheat drawn down on a covener, but the heat was real. Without any furnace, Zanne's bars would not hold their new shape for an hour. But an hour was enough.

They had worked out which makers had worked together to form the rings. Soon they found out how to feed them. No other attention was needed; to the joy of all three the beasts began to churn out new little rings. There should have been a hopper to catch them probably, like flour in the mill. It had gone; Sear's old bucket caught the bright shower instead.

Neither Sear nor Kest nor Zanne cared in the least that they were producing nothing at all. It was sheer pleasure to watch the makers making, strong and willing and noble as the ox that draws the plow. And the makers loved to do their work, too. Their shining happiness was clear in every movement.

Sear and Kest didn't worry too much about how the makers came to be. Kest liked marvels—especially marvels that were not produced by Covenant magic. He inquired no further. The simple old man probably really believed these were beasts with metal instead of flesh—no different from ten heifers in a barn. He tried to feed them sometimes, with baskets of rocks (he imagined metal might eat rock) and buckets of water.

But Zanne felt as if she had found what she had been looking for all her life. She was not interested in the naming of parts: the stepper, the governer, the worktable, the controller—names Sear dredged up out of old grandads' tales. What she saw was the principle at work under the forms. It was as if the people of the past had taken the laws of action that bind the world together and set them running on their own.

She wondered how they had been made to move before. She had never learned exactly how the people of the past achieved their marvels—before the Covenant. Such practical details didn't come into Uncle Lol's stories, and she couldn't remember that it had ever been explained at Hillen.

Sear knew. He showed her where at the foot of each beast a channel descended into the cave's floor.

"That's how it used ter come. It were all done by the old power from before the Covenant. There's a great big Maker far away out in the badlands. It's like the covener. In the olden days it would sent its power to all the makers in Mid-Inland. Like a river that's out o' sight."

Sear mumbled and he rambled. Kest had never paid attention beyond the first tale that had led him to the cave. He used the old man more like a servant now. But Zanne listened. Sear called the covener of this metal meeting "the Daymaker"—because as well as powering the makers, it was the source of the light in the towers. When the Day maker was awake there was no night in all Inland.

"Where is it?" asked Zanne.

"Ah. You take the ruin-road. Two wagon-halts past

70

Mosden, you takes the ruin road and it leads you out. And there 'ut be. At the end of all the roads."

"What does it look like, Sear? Is it a tower?"

But Sear turned shifty when she pressed him too hard.

"You'm making fun," he mumbled. "Ah ain't never been there. Tes just an old tale."

Zanne didn't know how far to believe the old man. But she found herself thinking often about the Daymaker. How wonderful it would be if the story was true. How wonderful to see Inland bathed in the light of neither sun nor moon, to hear the song of metal on metal everywhere.

When I am Teacher-Covener, she thought. I will use all my magic to search for places like this cave. I will be the one who teaches people how the wonderful past can come back.

Arles Townsend lost her orange trees. They died in a night, although it was Midsummer and all risk of frost was long over. Bren told her the news sorrowfully and they went out to look at the damage on a sweet summer morning, an hour or two after daybreak. Much of the foliage was still dark and glossy, but Arles felt that they were gone, beyond recall. The flowers were dead, half-grown fruit lay on the grass. She blamed that bridge above Mosden. The meetings up there must be drawing on the whole of Mid-Inland to get the road open again quickly. That's bad magic, grumbled Arles to herself. Wheeled travel is not a need. But oranges were also a luxury. It was just her fancy to grow those trees: a fancy that might be practical in another generation or two. They had always been on the edge of Garth's holding.

Then she turned her mind to the rest of the orchard, and saw that the grass under every tree was scattered with tiny green apples and pears.

Down in Garth village pensioners surveyed their gardens gloomily. It had been the same for days. Rosebuds that failed

71

to open, scented stock drooping, mean small flowers that either had no color at all or lost it in hours. The old people peered over each other's fences and were slightly mollified to find that everyone was suffering the same. This was the trouble with living in the country, they complained. The covener always put farming first. A bit of pleasure for those who'd worked all their lives went for nothing against the demands of some bean patch on bad soil that should never have been planted.

The innkeepers' children were playing on the Moss bridge. They balance walked along the parapet. Lant could do it with her eyes shut. Exel dared her to do it on her hands (with her eyes shut). Their little brother, waiting hopefully for one or other to fall in, lay in the road. He poked a stick into a hole he had found. Dust ran out. He discovered that the stones, under their overlay of packed earth, were pleasingly wobbly. The older girl and boy finally noticed what he was doing. They found that if they jumped up and down on the crown of the arch, the whole bridge seemed to shake. Excited, they ran home shouting.

The innkeepers were in their public room. Exel's father drew a beaker of beer from the new barrel. It was the second he had broached that morning. He took a mouthful and handed it to his wife. She filled her own mouth, and with a grimace of disgust went and spat into the innyard. She saw her children running across the great circle on the green, still battered and faded from the fleece harvest.

"Mother, Mother. The Moss bridge is falling down!"

Just as once before, when she helped her friends to run around Hillen in the shape of dreams, Zanne had not the slightest idea she was doing wrong. She had told herself at the start it wasn't the same as moving even a pebble that was under her mother's care. These creatures of the past didn't belong to Garth. And she believed she was using "her own" power. She was surprised that she didn't feel more tired. It must be because the makers had their own strength, even without that distant covener of theirs.

It was true, the makers had their strength. The same strength they had always had—to do their work and exact a price. Long ago the fuel that fed them had been taken from the earth in indirect ways. Now Zanne fed them by magic, but the power had to come from somewhere. Zanne drew on the world around her as she had once drained life and energy from her classmates, and didn't even know she was doing it. And just as long ago, it made no difference to the price that the makers were producing exactly nothing.

It was not meeting day, but the meetinghouse was full. On the speaker's platform under the cone of the roof, people had laid evidence of the sudden "blet," or blight. Withered flowers, tainted beer, unripe fruit fallen from the trees. A field of beans at Low had succumbed to mildew; an unpleasant cloying scent rose from a basket of ruined vines. There was also an empty milk pail. Liat of Bine End had brought in a tray of misshapen unusable pottery. Something had gone wrong with her kiln.

The people of Garth surveyed the evidence.

"Looks like we've got rats in the barn," said someone.

Zanne Townsend was not present, nor was Kest Upper Valley. Several people commented on their absence: and others laughed. Those two had been off together every day since fleece harvest. Too busy to notice if the whole valley was tumbling round their ears.

Just as at any Covenant meeting voices shuttled to and fro, and the covener waited for a natural pause before she started the day's business. But gossip was only on the surface today. The faces that looked to Arles were both angry and afraid.

"Covener, where is your Zanne?" asked Liat Bine End.

73

"We all felt the call to meeting. Surely you called her too—even if she has got a sweetheart."

"I called her," answered Arles grimly. "I called them both. But apparently they didn't hear me."

She had searched in her mind her holding and its environs. She knew the source of this "blet." She blamed herself for not spotting any warning signs before this. But now it was for the meeting to decide what should be done.

Zanne and Kest were with the makers. Old Sear had gone down to the river to fetch water and sand. Keeping his pets "fettled" was an endless pleasure to him. Zanne had been longing to take one of the makers apart. This angered Kest; he said she wanted to kill it. But she got her way in the end because without Zanne the treasure was dead meat anyway. So now they were working more or less together, with lamp oil and rather inadequate tools from Townsend barn. At the same time three of the other makers were racing away, cutting small toothed objects like little keys. The low room sang with their music; the great silver heads flashed to and fro with ceaseless easy energy.

There was a clattering and banging from the tunnel. Old Sear burst into the light. He stared around wild-eyed, clutching the decrepit bucket. He dropped the bucket, rushed into a corner and began throwing up slabs of decayed paneling, handfuls of dirt, all the time keeping up a high-pitched, inarticulate whimpering.

"Sear?" cried Zanne.

Kest jumped up.

"Hey, what's got into you, you old crazy?"

"They're coming!" howled Sear. "They're coming!"

He was still desperately flinging rubbish over the makers, Kest trying angrily to stop him, when the sound of tramping feet came down the tunnel and the door to the buried room was suddenly blocked with bodies. Faces of

74

stern women and angry men looked in, hands holding torches of wildfire. Zanne stood gaping. She saw her own mother and father in the crowd. The makers fell silent and still. She could not recognize the people of Garth. These were not her neighbors. This was a monster—many-headed and mindless.

Zanne had heard the lost past called evil. She had never taken that seriously. When Uncle Lol used to tell stories of the meat and sugar candy world she knew that was wicked waste—but it was only Lol's make-believe, and too long ago to be shocking. At Hillen the Tecovs only said, firmly, that the past was gone, beyond recall. They did not teach hatred. Zanne did not know that anger and fear were still alive.

In a way she was right. These were not the people she knew. They had become their own ancestors, facing again the horror of a world of marching towers and singing metal. Zanne's dream was their nightmare. The uncovenanted evil must be rooted out. The land must be cleansed.

Kest Upper Valley was taken by his mother, and by his uncle, who was Liat Bine End's husband. He fought them, shouting; others lent their hands. Zanne saw the strong young man borne down by brute weight of numbers. She saw old Sear fighting in a corner. No one touched her. She cried to her mother.

"Mother—stop them. They've gone crazy!"

"Move aside, my daughter," said Arles. She had an ax in her hand—not the little one from Townsend but a full-size tree-felling ax. She swung it with an effort above her head, and brought it crashing down.

Zanne screamed. Never in her life had she seen her mother destroy anything. Kill, yes, but never destroy.

But there in the flickering wildfire the beautiful makers died. They were not killed for meat or broken up in any way to be changed into other forms. They died uncovenanted and forever. After Arles the others came smashing and hammering with axes, with mallets, with anything that would do harm. That was only the beginning, a righteous expression of hatred. Next sacks of charcoal were brought in and other fuel, and gunpowder and a coil of fuse. Garth kept a small supply of such things, mostly unused nowadays but stored carefully in case of need. Arles used no magic. No covener would ever invoke that power for work done in fear and hatred.

The whole adult population of Garth gathered on the river beach downstream, and waited until a dull thud and a shaking of the rocks announced that the tunnel was blocked. Deep inside the fire would burn on, it had sufficient air. The contents of that cave would be reduced to heaps of twisted metal. They had left this place intact for too long, trusting a simple warding hold to keep off children and fools. No one had guessed actual makers were still whole inside the rubble heap. Garth would sleep easier now the sore was cleaned out.

Zanne was led away, by people she had known all her life and never known till now. She wouldn't look at them. She wept silently, and everyone thought she was ashamed and repentant. No one knew quite what to do with her. Little Zanne—so sunny and good. How could she have anything to do with such an ugly evil? The only way Garth could understand it was to put the blame on Kest. He was the older and always a troublemaker. It wouldn't be the first time a young woman had been led astray by a handsome sweetheart.

When Arles spoke to Zanne alone, she said much the same. She showed Zanne the evidence of how Garth had suffered when she brought the metal beasts to life.

She told her daughter, "Kest is a malcontent. He has a fine strong body and it runs away with him, making him think that all the world can be bent in his hand, like the strong man twisting horseshoes at a fair. There are always such people. Under the Covenant I will try to help him. Just as we'll all try to help crazy old Sear. But you shouldn't have done what you did to please any young stalwart. If you love him, you will have to change your ways with him."

"I don't love Kest," answered Zanne flatly. "I don't even like him much."

The idea of Kest as a sweetheart had hardly entered Zanne's head. She was going to be a Teacher-Covener. She had decided that, become sure of it, in the makers' company. Now she was sure of nothing.

"It was the makers I loved," she cried. "And you killed them."

They were in the kitchen at Townsend. Hurst and Bren had left the field to mother and daughter; they were keeping out of the way until the storm had passed. Night had fallen. The room was dimly lit by the one oil lamp allowed in this strict household. The sunstove was alight too, deep in its core; not for warmth but for reassurance after the troubles of the day. Zanne saw the faint rose glow that suffused those comfortable curves of earthenware. She saw the old rag rug at her feet. How faded it was now — worked by her mother's love, worked with bits of Townsend lives. Father's old jackets, pieces that had belonged to Grandmother Cutler, a red frock that once belonged to Bren when he still wore baby clothes and Zanne was hardly out of her cradle. Zanne had thought mother's magic was like that. A close warm patchwork wrapped around her to keep her safe forever. She remembered the night the raiders came in the snow. She remembered bloodstains on those homely colors, the day Uncle Lol was banished.

"They were beautiful," she whispered. "You hacked them up. Just because it's not your sort of power."

Arles said quietly, "Zanne, you do not understand. No

child can understand this. *Inland is made of magic.* The makers do not belong. They are dead as long as Inland lives. If they operate, Inland cannot be. I don't blame you for being shocked by the hate and fear you saw. But you see, those makers should be called takers. They do hard things quickly and easily, but that takes a lot of power. More than we can afford. You took the power out of Garth, by magic. Think if the blight had continued. Our fields starved and dead. All that we have built of beauty and comfort crumbling .... It cannot be helped. People will hate and fear something that threatens their very existence."

"They were alive. I know they were. You let their candle-flames go out."

After a little silence Arles sighed. She stood up, swept a handful of rotten beans and dead flowers from the table; took them and pushed them into the stove.

"I'm not going to talk to you any more, Zanne. I know very well there are things you can't listen to from your mother. Go back to Hillen, and your teachers. You'll learn. It's hard to have a talent larger than your understanding. I know that. You get confused by things that slower minds can't even see. You will learn. That's all I can say. Try not to be angry with me."

Zanne made no response. Only, when she got up to go to her room, she stopped at the door and turned round.

"I am sorry about the orange trees," she said.

The bridge on the Southway was repaired. Zanne traveled to Mosden the day before the northern wagons would set out. It was a sultry evening when she arrived at the house in Oldmarket Street, where Dimen's family lived. Dimen's parents were both Roadkeepers, their trade was to maintain the streets and roads. There was no sign of the work at home. No noisy shop or yard, no dirt. Only a narrow-fronted house of yellow stone, in a row of others just the same.

Zanne had stayed here before on her way back to Hillen. She visited the Roadkeepers turnabout with Grandma and Grandpa Weaver now. She was still shocked at the way they lived—the carpets on the floors, the elaborate meals; and especially their servants. But this time she let the houseboy take her cloak without protest, without remarking that it was a funny way to spend an apprenticeship.

The family dinner was served in a beautifully appointed dining room, with wall paintings of road-workers (in romantic poses and rich color) pretending to toil at their different tasks. It was a feast, as always on these occasions. To celebrate, Dimen commented dryly, the fact that they're getting rid of me again. Zanne ate steadily and hardly spoke a word. Dimen's father had a sharp, though kindly tongue. He always teased the little covenanter; and she always gave back as good as she got, in a bright and sunny style that pleased the townsman. But this time he could hardly raise a smile from her.

Dimen's mother liked to think she was as knowledgeable about magic as she was about the state of Mosden's cobbled streets. From her great knowledge, she found plenty to criticize. Zanne could change like quicksilver—like a covener indeed—and respond to the somewhat self-important Roadkeeper without offence but with uncompromising dignity. Tonight she said "Yes" and "No" like an awkward child. She was like a candle with the flame blown out. If Dimen had not known better, she would have thought someone was dead at Townsend.

The two girls shared a room. The house was immensely luxurious, but public and communal rooms took up most of its space. Mosden Oldmarket meeting controlled the "floormeasure" for each citizen with a strictness unknown in the countryside. Zanne retired early. Dimen followed her. She found the younger girl kneeling on her bed with her

Hillen box open: sorting rapidly, almost furtively, through the contents. Zanne didn't speak. Her face was pale and drawn, she looked ill. Dimen went to sit on the painted windowseat. It struck her as odd that Zanne hadn't even opened the window—she who always complained that she was suffocated by the close air of the town.

"Zanne," she coaxed. "Let's go for a walk by the river. It's almost dark; it will be cooler down there. You can sort your things at Hillen."

"I'm not going back to school."

"*Not going back to school?*"

"No. I'm going out into the badlands. I have to look for something there."

She spoke so briskly and calmly that Dimen started to laugh. She thought it was a joke.

Zanne shook her head.

"I mean it, Dimen. I'm going. You don't have to come if you don't want to."

"Me?" gasped Dimen. "What have I got to do with this?"

"Well—that's up to you."

Then she told Dimen the story of the makers. And as always Dimen was caught up in Zanne's excitement, was amazed at the discovery of the metal beasts; was horrified at the people of Garth, turned into a mindless mob by their fear of the past.

"But why do you have to go to the badlands?"

"Because that's where the Daymaker is. The source of the power that people used before the Covenant. It was wrong of me to steal from Garth to feed the makers. But this other power isn't magic—where you can't move a leaf without upsetting the whole world. Mother doesn't understand. All she knows is Covenant magic. She can't imagine something that works differently."

Zanne continued her sorting.

"We take the ruin-road," she went on confidently. "From the second wagon-halt past Mosden. The Daymaker is at the end of that road. I'm not sure what it looks like, but I'll recognize it. It'll be like the makers, and they were like nothing else in the world."

Dimen put her elbows on her knees and propped her chin on her fists, gazing at her friend with something between admiration and fascinated horror.

"What about the raiders, Zanne?"

Zanne had been thinking about the raiders. She was reminded of her Uncle Lol. Lol hadn't vanished completely when he walked away from Townsend, five years ago. Mother heard from him occasionally. He was in south Inland, the last anybody knew, down on the seacoast. She remembered, impatiently brushing aside the ugly part of the story for now, that her uncle had been friends with some outlaws. They couldn't be all bad.

"We probably won't meet them. And if we do, why should they hurt us? We've got nothing for them to steal. Oh, Dimen, I don't know if I can even wake the Daymaker. Or how to use it to bring back the past. But I have to try. Don't you see? Then everyone will have all the things we can't have now, because there isn't enough magic. Shoes in summer, smooth roads. Lights all night outside every house. . ."

Dimen burst out laughing.

"For a Garth valley covenanter," she exclaimed, "you certainly are full of surprises, Zanne!"

She knew that she would have to go along. It was quite clear that she could not make Zanne give up the idea: equally clearly she could not enlist her parents. They would shut Zanne up and send officious word to Townsend. Dimen burned with shame at the idea—an apprentice covener must not be treated like that. No, Zanne would set off for the badlands, leaving Dimen to arrive alone at Hillen and explain things to Holder Elima. She did not relish that prospect. It would be much simpler to join the expedition. It was quite clear to Dimen that Zanne didn't actually know what a "Daymaker" was. Or what she would do with one if she found it. But that problem, thought the older girl wisely, was not likely to trouble them. Most likely they would not find anything. But the attempt would heal Zanne's injured pride. And it couldn't do any harm.

It was raining when their wagon team set them down, at the second stop out of Mosden. There was a small carriers' inn, a flint track that led off into farmland on the left, and on the right the forest. No settlement was in sight. But opposite the flint track, in a tangle of weeds, was the opening of a broad treeless ride. The wagoners' girl sat dangling her bare muddy feet over the tailgate and stared insolently.

"How far is it to the Outlands?" demanded Zanne.

"Dunno." The girl didn't look interested. "'Bout thirty vale."

The clumsy vehicle lumbered off on its way.

"Thirty vales!" groaned Dimen. "Oh, I wish I could get hold of that covener who let the bridge fall down. If it hadn't been for her, none of this would have happened."

But sweet summer rain danced on the cobbles of the inn yard, and the air was fresh with promise.

"Look—"

Zanne pointed to a bright patch of blue sky.

"The sun's coming out for us. That's sure to be a good sign."

# CHAPTER 5

TO WALK INTO Mosden forest—green and sunlit, shining with rain and shouting with birdsong—was to enter a world almost as unknown to Zanne as to townbred Dimen. When Zanne used to play in Garth beechwoods or go nutting in a hazel coppice on the edge of the fields, roads and other farming valleys were always around her. Not many people ever entered the true forest that stretched here, north of Mosden, right to the borders of Inland. The fear of raider bands and of dangerous animals kept them away. And also the wildwood had its own Covenant, that neither wanted or needed ordinary human compnay.

But though animals and birds were strangely shy, the forest did not seem very hostile, and Zanne had confidence in her quest. The ride was thoroughly overgrown and not very easy walking. The two girls marched purposefully along its line, following deer paths and taking care to break and disturb as little as possible. Dimen felt safer off the outlaw road (although raiders couldn't have used this one for years) and Zanne didn't mind. It was easy enough to keep that break in the trees in sight.

Squirrels chattered at them. Deer started from the under growth and leapt away, flying over the brambles like skimmed pebbles with their legs tucked up and white rumps flashing. They walked under dizzying arches of honeysuckle, skirted wet bottoms carpeted with pungent, fading wild garlic. Mostly they went in silence. The trees did not seem to want to listen to human voices.

They had sent a letter on with their boxes to Hillen, telling Holder Elima that Zanne of Garth had decided to make her choice journey and Dimen of Mosden went with her. This was Dimen's idea and quite a plausible excuse. There was no ceremony attached to the start of that wandering time. A young woman just made up her own mind and set out.

Zanne had been uneasy about the deception. The decision should come out of the journey and hers was already made. She would never be a Teacher-Covener. At least not any kind of Tecov that Hillen could imagine. But Dimen persuaded her. In fact, though she had more sense than to say so, the older girl believed there was no deception involved. Zanne had been hurt and upset by the destruction of her makers. For the first time she had felt the web of magic and duty, that had bound her all her young life, as a cage—a constriction. She saw a choice where there had been no choice before. She needed time and space to think things out. That was how Dimen saw it.

And now Zanne was glad that she had agreed to write that note. She didn't want anyone to be worried, but she certainly didn't want anyone to know what was happening until the Daymaker was restored. She strode through the trees feeling free and empty, as if she'd put down some enormous burden, and the vagrant's pack on her back seemed more like a pair of wings.

After a while they stopped by a stream to fill their water bottles. They unloaded and repacked their packs more rationally. This was a disappointing experience. Dimen had brought soap, a little roll of coined money and several other small useful items. But she would have eaten inn food on the journey to school and had no provisions except a bag of delicacies, picked out of the box her parents' cook had put up to enliven the Hillen diet. Zanne was loaded with sensible dry rations from Townsend larder. Besides these, she had brought only a change of clothes and her moonlamp.

They each carried a water bottle and the stout waterproof cloak that was essential for any Inland journey even in high summer. They had one beaker between them, no knife, no cooking pots, no way of striking wildfire except by magic.

So they laughed in despair, and ate a spiced custard roll which was already beginning to escape from its oilpaper wrapping. It was meant for six but it was taking up too much room anyway. It tasted wonderful. So did the water, flavored faintly with moss and leaf mold.

At dusk they were still walking. The rain had blown away somewhere outside the wood and a moon rose before the end of the long twilight. Its glow was sufficient to light a path—until at last they found the white disk overhead in a clearing made by one giant oak. They felt they had covered about seven vales from the road. It was enough for half a day. They decided to camp.

Zanne sat down on the moss under the oak. All at once her spirits had plunged.

The moon was slightly on the wane but very bright. The clearing was black and white, each shadow sharply defined, not like the dappled sunlight where everything was confused and one person's opinion as good as another's.

"Things look different by moonlight, don't they," she murmured.

All her life she had known that beyond Mosden forest the Outlands began. That and no more. Nobody went out there, except the raiders. But she and Dimen would not lose their way. Zanne knew now that that was impossible. She could feel two directions pulling inside her—toward Inland, and away from Inland. They had only to walk exactly the way that seemed most wrong, and that would lead them straight along the route of Sear's old ruin-road. She looked at Dimen, anxiously, wondering if her friend had the same feeling. It was madness, really, for them to set out like this. But she would not say so.

"Let's do our Link," suggested Dimen. "We'll feel better for it in the morning."

She was glad when Zanne agreed. It was fun to be on a quest. But it didn't seem right to see the sturdy little covenanter abandoning all her duties. Using a jutting root for a barre and leaf litter for a floor mat, the two girls stretched and reached and curled; exercising the supple strength driven into them in long painful hours under the Mound.

They knew they were being watched. They thought it was the presence of the forest itself they felt, until four slim figures detached themselves from the dark under the trees. Dimen dropped her pose and quickly lifted her moonlamp from the pack near her feet. It was a market trinket, made in a Mosden tradeshop. But it glowed as bright as Zanne's pebble. The four strangers wore the prick-eared masks of wolves. They were armed like outlaws and scantily dressed in animal skins. But they knew the lamp.

One of the savages came forward, pulling off her wolf mask, her eyes glinting topaz under a shaggy mane of hair. She touched the light with fingers that had long curved nails like claws.

"Covenant," she said. And then, haltingly, "You are strangers in the wood. Why are you here? You must come with."

The girls protested but it was no use. They had passed too close to a forest settlement, and they must explain themselves to the covener.

The village was in an open glade nearby. The summer

86

cabins were no more than heaps of bracken humped on stakes. They looked like big long-legged animals sleeping on their feet in the moonlight. Foresters gathered around, questioning the wolf girls in a dialect Dimen and Zanne could barely recognize. They touched the girls' clothes and packs censoriously; most of them were naked except for a kilt of leather or green tradecloth.

"This reminds me," hissed Dimen, "of the day I arrived in Garth."

"Sssh! It isn't funny!"

The covener was not present. She was away in some other part of her holding. The two strangers must wait for her return.

The foresters were a strange people. They had no use for towns or farms. Occasionally their flores left the wood to take up a normal trade. But otherwise there was no contact between them and the rest of Inland, except when they dragged sledges of timber and skins out to trading points on the wagon roads. Zanne had not forgotten about them. But foresters were supposed to be shy and wary. She had hoped she and Dimen would manage to get by without crossing tracks with the keepers of the wood.

It was extremely galling, to be stopped like this almost within hailing distance of Mosden. Dimen managed to find the accident amusing, but Zanne fretted. The foresters did not even feed their guests—or at least not very well. They said it was the girls' own idea to come into the wood. It had made no Covenant to support them.

After three days the covener returned. Sahan, the wolf girl who had made herself responsible for the travelers, came to fetch Dimen and Zanne at twilight. The covener was waiting for them under a great sweet chestnut in the middle of the glade. A spread of pale grass-woven mats made the floor of this meetinghouse; there were no walls.

She was an old woman with a dark, seamed face, gray eyes, and silver braids of hair. She looked as wild as the rest but Zanne knew this was deceptive. This aged savage had spent her years under the Mound once. Perhaps she'd never even been a forester at all, until Hillen Coven sent her where she was needed.

"Well," said the old lady, in a tone neither warm nor cool. "Town girl, farm girl. Hillen students both, I hear. What is your business so deep in our land?"

Zanne swallowed hostility. She knew the rights of the forest. She and Dimen could be escorted back to the road now: like ignorant townfolk shooed out of a field of young grain.

A covener would not read Zanne's mind, not in the forbidden way. This woman could not know she was talking to someone determined to restore the makers. It was just as well. For obviously a covener of the forest would be the last person to sympathize with that quest. Zanne looked at the great barley sugar—twisted bole of the sweet chestnut. The foresters' meetinghouse was a tree that was no use as timber; a tree that couldn't be made into beams or planks or tables or chairs. Zanne took the point. And she was afraid. Surely this wise woman would sense the threat to her ways. At the least, undoubtedly she could read faces. She would know if someone was lying.

"We are Zanne of Garth and Dimen of Mosden. Continuers. I am making my choice journey, my friend keeps me company."

"Sit down."

The bright eyes studied them carefully.

"I see from your clothes and your manner that this journey is scarcely begun. The Covenant must have led you here. Someone should question you before you go further. The impulse to wander is a tricky thing. One can be mistaken."

Zanne felt, bitterly, as if she was in Holder Elima's study.
"What is on your backs? Do you have cooking gear?"
"N-no."
"Do you have a strike-a-light?"
"None."
"How did the idea of the journey come to you? Was it long prepared?"
"I—something happened. And I just had to go."
"Where are you going? And what do you hope to find?"
"Toward the east, to the badlands. And I—I don't want to tell you."
That was the worst. The covener's eyes were without expression, inward turned. There was a long pause, in which Dimen tried not to hold her breath. At last the old woman sighed. She took Zanne's hands in hers, which were dark as dead leaves, with long and broken nails.
"Do you know what it means, child, to go to the badlands? To the Outlands, beyond our borders?"
"I know it will be dangerous," said Zanne, trying to sound like a responsible traveler.
"Very dangerous, Zanne."
The covener's grip on Zanne's hands was lizard dry and very strong. Her eyes made Zanne shiver. Was her mind being read after all? But at last the woman released her, smiling a little.
"Yes. That is the way it begins. From one moment to the next. Drop your hand from the plow and walk away. You are not deceived, Zanne. You are indeed facing the choice of your life. And you must face it wandering and lost, there is no other way. The forest will let you pass—to reach this goal which you don't want to talk about."
Zanne flushed and ducked her head. She was ashamed. The old covener looked beyond her, at Dimen standing anxiously by. She frowned a little.

"However, I add this, young woman who does all the talking. A choice journey is better made alone. The Covenant seems to tell me you should consider that."

Zanne and Dimen went back to their shelter, a roof of green bracken on a frame of larch boles, which they shared with three forester girls. Zanne could not sleep for excitement. Her uncertainty of the moon glade was gone. Why should the forest covener be so easily won over, if not because the Covenant itself was on Zanne's side? They had the foresters' protection now which would speed the journey. This delay had been a good thing after all. But as for leaving Dimen behind, that couldn't be good advice. It just wouldn't be fair.

The next day, Sahan the wolf girl was their guide. She told them, using the common language of Inland, that she was destined for Hillen herself.

"I will go there—at Leafall. Oh, I can hardly bear it. To live underground. I won't be a wolf anymore; I will be a fat old badger."

She asked if Hillen students always wore so many clothes, even in summer. Dimen solemnly assured her that this was the shocking truth—and she laughed in scandalized amazement.

Sahan showed them things they would never have seen alone. She told them how hard the foresters worked, how everything in the wood, though it looked so untouched, was tended and bathed in magic like the fields of Garth. But she did not actually speed their journey much. There were too many diversions to avoid areas where humans must not intrude, too many paths that must not be trodden except by the wild creatures that made them. She tried to make Dimen take off her polluting town shoes, but that proved totally impractical.

Zanne accepted Sahan's diversions patiently. But she was

puzzled to notice that they were being followed. Several times she glimpsed someone watching them: a woman, tall, and wearing her hair wild and long in the forest way. Obviously the covener didn't trust "town girl and farm girl" to behave themselves. Finally, she challenged Sahan.

"Who is that woman following us?"

Sahan looked surprised. Just then they were walking through an open glade of beeches. The forest woman was clearly visible behind them, walking silently and gracefully; a wreath of green leaves in her hair.

"Look—there she is."

Sahan looked back. She said, after a moment,

"I see no woman."

"But—"

"And neither do you."

Sahan's expression was so serious Zanne didn't argue. She realized that she was up against the strange ways of the foresters.

At nightfall Sahan found them a place to sleep in long soft grass between a thicket of hazels and a stream. She told them they would find the old road if they dropped south now about half a vale, but advised them to stay away from it as long as they could. The forest paths were safer, as long as the forest lasted.

"The outlaws use that road, to come hunting. And they do not always wait for winter." She couldn't tell them anything about the land beyond. "We never go there" was all she would say.

There was no need for a fire. They sat in the shadows, talking softly and laughing: sharing a meal of fancy Mosden food. Suddenly Zanne was aware that something had joined them. For a moment she thought, *it's a leopard* because she had the feeling of something very wild and strange, watching her. And then the forest woman whom she had seen earlier stepped out of the shadows, and sat down.

At the time it seemed quite natural. Sahan greeted the forester with great respect, as if she were a covener. She called the stranger "Chestnut" and told her all about Zanne and Dimen, as if she had a right to know.

Chestnut's arms and legs were ruddy and smooth. She wore a kilt of fresh leaves; leaves and twigs were tangled in her hair. She listened, and nodded; and then she came to Dimen and gave her something. Dimen understood it was a token, a sign of protection. She thought Chestnut said: *Remember me, Dimen, in the Outlands where there are no trees. And I will remember you.*

But then the woman was gone. The hazel thicket was empty but for themselves. Zanne and Dimen looked at each other uncertainly, in the glow of Zanne's moonlamp; and Dimen was holding in her palm a horse chestnut, glowing fresh and new as if it was Leafall now, not Midsummer.

"Don't be frightened," whispered Sahan. "In the forest we meet those people sometimes. Maybe our magic makes them, maybe they *are* and magic lets us meet them. No one knows. . . ."

Dimen stared. "But this chestnut's real."

"Yes. You must keep it, Dimen. I think it will protect you from any harm. At least while you are in our land."

Sahan left them too then, making them promise they would come back this way and see her again. At any rate they would meet at Hillen, in Leafall. She put on her wolf mask and vanished into the darkness. She was not tired and there was nothing for her to fear in a walk through the forest night.

"Well!" exclaimed Dimen. "So I've been talking to a tree, have I? I'm glad my poor mama can't see me. This'd confirm all her worst fears about sending me to magic school."

For two more days they walked on. On the first, they still

saw signs of the forest Covenant: trees where dead or damaged wood had been cut away, drainage channels, young saplings growing inside thickets of thorn to keep off the squirrels and deer. They saw no foresters, no wolves; and not even a pawprint of the rare but dangerous Inland leopard. There didn't seem to be many animals or birds about at all. On the second day things did not go so well. Sahan had given them no guidance for this stage. And now the forest was no longer tended. Fallen trees blocked the paths. Thorny vines climbed up into overhanging branches in impenetrable curtains. Mounds of bramble seemed to hide solid shapes and formed impassable obstacles. The forest floor was breaking up into murky pools and weedfilled holes. It was backbreaking work to make a way through, and it rained all day and they had no fire.

At one point Zanne stumbled onto the barren ride. They had been walking parallel to it, after leaving its line in a long curve the day they walked with the forest girl. Zanne was taken by surprise. She was alarmed to think she had started heading south without knowing it. She called to Dimen, and they both stepped out into the open. It was a relief to be under the sky again. But it was a gray sky, and the ancient road had changed. It was still overgrown but obviously in use. There was rubbish on it—rusty bits of metal, greasy piles of rags and bones, human and horse dung lying in the trodden way.

"I don't think we can use this," whispered Dimen. "It doesn't feel safe."

It occurred to both of them that if Sear's trail was so dangerous even within the forest, things weren't going to get any better. And it was the only clue they had, to lead them to Zanne's Daymaker. However, neither of them spoke. Dimen was waiting hopefully for Zanne to give up of her own accord. Zanne's determination was as strong as ever.

The next day was no better. Another dull sky, and under it the forest itself seemed to be turning gray. They made hardly any progress at all. The trees were so thickly grown with lichen and creepers their foliage was sparse even now, in high summer. Many of them seemed to be dead standing up; more than once Zanne or Dimen grabbed a branch for support and found the whole tree coming away in their hands. The dried-blood color of newly exposed dead wood seemed to be the only color left.

Dimen collapsed on a rotten stump.

"I'm worn out," she announced. "Let's eat."

There was no path here but the one they'd broken for themselves. And in spite of the violence, it seemed to have closed up behind them without a sign. All around were rusty brambles, and dead trees sheeted with last year's clematis in ghostly drifts of gray. Zanne sat with her back to a mound of indistinguishable rubbish.

"Has it occurred to you," remarked Dimen, "that the whole of the Outlands could be like this?"

"That's not what people say. They say it is empty and bare."

"People don't come here. And I must say I don't blame them."

Zanne looked back into the ground they'd covered that morning. At least, she hoped she was looking back. It was uncannily difficult to tell, with no sun in the sky and no visible path. This dismal thicket that had taken over from Inland's wild wood was not trustworthy. It could do anything—shift its shape, melt away, or thicken like fog.

"My head aches," complained Dimen. "It's the heat, I think."

Zanne looked at her friend sharply. She had just been wishing she didn't feel so chilly.

Suddenly she made a decision. Up till this point they had

used no magic except the moonlamps. They had been going step by step like good Hillen girls. Continuers are not supposed to meddle with the real world.... But she had already broken that rule, more than once. And she meant to do much more. It was simply silly to go on being obedient to Hillen now, just out of habit.

"Dimen, I'm going up to have a look around. Maybe I'll be able to see a way forward."

Dimen was munching a piece of savory Townsend bean-bread. It tasted as if it had begun to go moldy.

"Up? What do you mean? None of these trees looks solid enough for climbing."

"No, and they're not tall enough either. I will have to lift."

Dimen felt she should protest. But she told herself philosophically there was no point in starting an argument she was bound to lose.

"Do you think you can do it? The atmosphere here—it isn't like a magic studio."

"I can do it."

Zanne gobbled up the last of her bread. She kicked around in the rubbish until she had a clear patch of earth. She balanced herself: knees flexed, arms above her head—and dived upward into the air.

"Keep your head in line!" shouted Dimen. "Unlock your shoulders—"

But already Zanne, laughing at her own ease, was level with the highest branches of the stunted trees.

The dive carried her for half a breath. She pulled her arms back and lifted herself again: straight upward, not attempting any forward motion. No one could maintain that for long, not even a child prodigy. There were legendary coveners, old and paper-light bodies, who could lift and then glide on the air currents like great birds. Zanne didn't try. She didn't want to land lost in the tangle, and anyway the air was flat and still. She looked down between her feet and saw Dimen absurdly foreshortened, waving her arms cheerfully. Beyond Dimen the thickets continued. In one direction they changed from gray to green again. In another, to the east, the tangle went on, growing lower and more broken until all the trees were gone.

And beyond, she saw the Outlands. Gray, sand color, rust red, and opaque places like patches of heat haze. She saw Sear's "ruin-road" coming out of the thicket and joining up with a maze of other tracks, like a tangle of pale worms wriggling across the gray plain.

Zanne closed her eyes and pushed. She didn't like the look of that maze. But the Daymaker must be identifiable in some way. She must get higher. When she opened her eyes, her head was buzzing dangerously. She looked down. What she saw astonished her. The waste went on. It was bare ground she saw, but nothing like a plowed field. This was stripped and scoured—not earth, only dust. She saw it moving in places like water. She saw jagged shapes, tiny in the distance, and knew she was seeing ruined towers, like the ruins of those towers that had once covered Garth valley. She could see no end. She looked back, and there was Inland. But it had changed; it had withered away. She could see now, as if clear over the sheep downs, to where the waste began again. And the forest shrinking and dwindling northward until the road from Mosden was a thin trickle of green, and the waste on either side vast and borderless....

She held herself at that height, until a numbness in her feet and hands and heaviness in her belly gave her warnings she could not ignore. And then fell. Spiraling downward, downward, into the murky and broken canopy.

She landed on her feet, lightly, and at once collapsed, burying her head between her knees. Dimen, who had been watching with mounting anxiety, hurried to wrap a cloak around her cold shoulders. She held the beaker to Zanne's lips; the girl drank with chattering teeth. It was fruit syrup, sweet and hot.

Dimen grinned.

"You're not the only one who can break the rules."

Zanne gulped, only able to nod her thanks.

"Did you see a way? Did you see the Daymaker?"

The younger girl didn't reply. She was shaking all over. Dimen spread the other cloak.

"All right, don't try to talk. You have to rest and get warm. As many hours to recover as you take breaths in the air, you know the rule."

When she turned around. Zanne was on her feet. The cloak was slipping off her shoulders. She was tugging at a sheet of some hard but flexible material that jutted out of the undergrowth.

"Zanne—"

"I'll rest later," declared Zanne. "We can't stay here. It—it's too horrible."

She did not say what was too horrible. She went on tugging and pulling at bits of rubbish. At first Dimen helped her, thinking she must be trying to clear a path. But her friend's actions made no sense. She stood back and watched in bewilderment.

A pile of junk gathered. The broad flexible sheet: some long pipes, some strange disk shapes. All day they had been wandering through these overgrown heaps of refuse. Zanne had not noticed before how odd it was to find a giant rubbish dump, here on the edge of nowhere. She touched the stuff and felt its strangeness. Neither wood nor stone nor skin, nor metal out of the rock.... Her eyes grew wide. When she was a little girl, she had imagined that if you followed a ruin-road it might lead you back through time. Was that true? Stuff that had rotted into Inland earth long ago was still whole here on

97

the borders. What if the towers of light really were still standing, somewhere out there? But she remembered the waste of emptiness she had just seen. She decided she would work out the puzzle later. Now, the important thing was to move on.

Dimen was thinking that the rubbish should have been crawling with woodlice and worms. It was not. She wasn't excessively fond of creepy-crawlies, but she would have welcomed an honest slug or two now. But Zanne apparently felt no revulsion. She knelt beside her mad arrangement, still shivering and wan faced but alert and determined.

"Did you see outlaws?"

"No. It's—it looks like a long way to the end of the road."

She paused, adjusting the pipes, and the springy wedges that propped them up.

"We can't walk so far."

Dimen was mystified.

"What is it? A kind of sculpture? It looks a bit like a boat."

"That's what it is. A flying boat." She laughed shakily. "I'm going to call it Junk."

She stroked the lines of her creation. She had copied the only boats she knew well, the flat-bottomed punts that Garth people used on the Moss meadows in a spring flood. It had a square forefoot, a hooped shelter behind just big enough for two. The stern had a steering oar with a flattish paddle, and it was raised so the person steering could see ahead. Zanne had shaped nothing. She had searched for fragments that suited her, and they came to hand willingly. She knew the rubbish was glad to be in use again. She thought of the red deer in the forest, how they tucked up their legs and floated over the brambles.

Up rose the good ship Junk and settled itself together, hovering at waist height. The shelter gathered itself and became rigid. The oar waggled in the air; Junk heeled over and then steadied itself, upright. It was as if a large animal had just walked into the clearing and stood looking at them with the benign ponderous curiosity of a herd of cows. Dimen approached, handled the boat's sides, walked around it. Her distaste had gone now. The ugly stuff was alive. Somehow Zanne had made it feel right and magical.

"Don't you find it hard?" she asked, "—working with these nasty things?"

"No," answered Zanne blankly.

"Ugh—I would."

Zanne put her hand on the gunwale and coaxed Junk to the ground. They stowed their packs and climbed on board.

"What did you see, Zanne? You haven't told me yet. Where are we heading for now?"

"It's a bit confusing," said Zanne, as Junk began to move. She compressed her lips as if afraid to say more. "I saw sort of fields." She pointed ahead of them. "There are people living over there. They'll help us."

At which point, without fuss, she quietly folded up into the bottom of the boat in a dead faint. Junk was pattern-magic, like the knife that became a river for the legendary Covener of Kor. The unity between the odd craft and a boat, between water and air, did not depend on Zanne. She only recognized it—with a depth of conviction that was her magic talent. But she had used her own physical strength for the lift, and the price had to be paid.

"Oh no," groaned Dimen. She grabbed at the swinging oar. "Oh no—"

Zanne's last memory was of falling. She thought she had fallen from the air. She lay still, letting herself recover. She was thinking of what she had seen from her lift. She had thought Inland was the whole world. When she came to want to escape, she thought it was hardly possible. But she had seen a fragile thing, a thin web of knots and strands of life, spread over a great dead mass. She kept her eyes closed. She did not know how much she had seen from her height in the air and how much from a different sense. She remembered, Inland had no maps. Not since the long ago. Its contours, its variations were known, but no one wanted to think of its limits. Perhaps now she understood why.

She became aware of a rocking motion. The moment she noticed this and began to worry about it, the motion stopped with a jolt and a jar. She saw Dimen kneeling opposite her, clutching the steering oar. She remembered making Junk. The boat was grounded, but still intact.

"Where are we?" she asked hoarsely.

"I think we're in a field."

They climbed out. Dusk was gathering (surely very early for high summer?). Junk had landed itself on a path through a field of grain. Dimen thought it was wheat. Even to her ignorant eyes the stalks looked thin and yellowy, the heads meager. But perhaps it was the murky twilight that made everything look so sickly.

Carrying both their packs, with Zanne leaning on her arm, Dimen followed the path toward a collection of low buildings. She found herself in an open square of trodden earth. There was rubbish and filth on the ground as on the outlaws' road. People came out of dark doorways. They looked as sickly as the grain to the Inland girl. They kept their distance, staring rudely.

"Is your covener here?"

Dimen mentally apologized to the foresters. They weren't savages at all.

"If she's not here, it doesn't matter. We only want rest and shelter."

Someone laughed. It was a young man. He sidled forward, grinning. He was obviously the village zany, thought Dimen. She gave him the smile one gives to people who set themselves up to be fools. That made him cackle with delight, and then in a moment the rest of them moved in. Dimen was surrounded by jeering, hostile faces. Something hard and stinging smacked her cheek. The little girls at the back were throwing stones.

Zanne was no help. Her head had fallen on Dimen's shoulder; she was out on her feet. But Mosden had its share of uncouth individuals, like any town. Dimen shouted, with her mother's harsh authority.

"Get away from me!"

They got.

Still glaring at the crowd she slipped her pack down her arm, groped in it and brought out her moonlamp. It flashed, reflecting the brightness of her anger.

"There now. See—we're not raiders. This is Covenant magic. Now will you be civil?"

She spoke to the empty square. The villagers, one and all, had vanished.

It was only by peering into a doorway and forcing herself on the goggle-eyed creatures within, that she managed to get herself and Zanne a place to stay. Even then she had to pay, in coined Mosden metal. These people had no idea of the simple rights of a traveler.

She secured a one-room cottage with an earth floor. There were some boards in a corner to sleep on. The hovel was built very badly, partly of rough planks and partly of weird old refuse. Zanne collapsed, wrapped in two wagon cloaks. Her face was gray, her skin felt cold and moist. Dimen found a chip of stone in the rubbish at her door, and started to dig in the packed earth. She was preparing a sunstove. If they were going to break Hillen rules, it might as well do them some good. This was one magic, she reflected, that Zanne couldn't manage. She might be a prodigy but she wasn't a woman yet.

101

The door, which was a curtain of musty damp felt, was pushed aside. The young man who played village idiot came in. He peered around, looking with great interest at Dimen's moonlamp, and the red glow curled in the center of a small hole grubbed in the ground.

"What do you want?" snapped Dimen.

"Want bread," whined the zany.

He held out his hand, cowed and cringing like a dog that has been beaten in a fight. Dimen was disgusted. There were no beggars in Inland. She could hardly believe in someone who wanted for bread.

"Here." She hauled a generous chunk off a Townsend loaf. "Now stop playing the fool."

Zanne sat up suddenly. "Clear off!" she shouted. "Get out of here!"

The man shuffled out, examining his prize with a sulky expression.

"Want *white* bread—"

Dimen was shocked. "There was no need to shout, Zanne."

"You shouldn't have let him in. He was spying, didn't you see?"

"But suppose he was really hungry?"

"I don't believe it," mumbled Zanne, burying her head again. "Anyway, we need all our food. Can't give it away...."

They were halted again, and this time it was Zanne's fault. It was obvious that she would need days of rest to recover from that reckless lift. But in any case it would have been hard for the girls to leave this village speedily. Once the people realized their visitors had Covenant magic, there was a constant trail of suppliants. A burned hand, oozing under dirty bandages, a colicky baby, a set of carpenter's tools, badly made and disobedient in the hand. Some scraggy chickens with a nasty scale complaint. Dimen and Zanne became coveners overnight. It was hard work. There was no one for them to turn to. They must decide for themselves when to shift and when to hold; how to achieve one thing without undoing several others.

The village had no name that Zanne or Dimen could discover. The people spoke their own dialect; communication with them was mostly by signs. They did not know what it meant to have a covener, and looked on schoolgirl magic with awe. And yet Dimen, exploring, found some sheds where a good number of horses had been stabled not too long ago. In Inland, horses were luxury. The villagers were not rich; they were very poor. Dimen did not mention this puzzle to their hosts. She thought she could work it out for herself. The outlaw road passed close by these hovels.

When Zanne was well, the Hillen girls insisted on being taken out to the fields. There was earth underfoot, and the sun and moon of summer were hidden somewhere in the gray clouds. They did their best for the struggling crops; there should be some increase at harvest time. The villagers were mystified by this tour. They only knew of magic as a peddler's art of mending and doctoring. Soon only a straggle of children was left of the harvest meeting, and they melted away when nothing exciting happened. The girls went to Junk, which was safe and untouched; the villagers were too wary to meddle with it.

"We must get away soon," said Zanne.

They had discussed the evidence Dimen had found. Raiders obviously made use of this village. And now, out here in the wilderness, Zanne was less than confident about the friendliness of those people. On the edge of the fields there was a long line of rubble heaps and massive standing blocks, a kind of wall. The villagers said this wall had been built by their ancestors. The real Outlands started on the other side. They would have to cross this barrier, and go on following Sear's road from a distance, as they had done through the forest. Zanne had not yet told Dimen about the maze she had seen from the air. She was hoping there would be some new clue to follow, beyond the wall.

On the way back to the hovels there was a wide black ditch. It ran strongly but looked very dirty.

"We've been drinking this," remarked Dimen. "We've been *paying* for it."

Water is the most difficult element, even for full coveners. She took the forester token from her pocket. She had grown fond of her chestnut. But they had left the forest now, and the villagers' need was greater. She dropped it into the stream.

"That's all I've got left. Hope it does some good. I feel as if someone had picked me up by the heels and shaken all the magic out."

"Me, too."

They looked back over the miserable fields.

"Imagine being placed in a settlement like this! It could happen, I suppose."

"No, it couldn't." Zanne shook her head, wonderingly. "This is not Inland. This isn't our country at all. We are outside the world."

# CHAPTER 6

JUNK SAILED AWAY, from grateful smiles and a farewell gathering of screeching children. But Zanne had been right to be suspicious of that sturdy beggar. The borderland people did not raid Inland themselves (except when times were really hard). However, they lived in fear of the outlaws, who were the harsh rulers of this land, and a short unofficial visit from Hillen couldn't change that. When Zanne and Dimen set out into the open waste, carefully avoiding the outlaw road, news of their quest had already traveled ahead.

It had been impossible to find out anything concrete about the Daymaker. One scrawny young woman vowed she had seen it, once when she was on a scavenging hunt far beyond the wall. It was all covered with light, like the thing Dimen had in her pocket. But she couldn't decide if the object she'd seen was as big as a house, or the same size as a moonlamp. So Zanne reluctantly had to discount that story. One thing was sure though. The word was recognized. Eyes brightened, with fear and a kind of hunger, when Zanne started asking questions. And those who spoke a little of the ordinary Inland language said that was a great magic, the Daymaker. Older and greater than your power from the Fatland. But it is lost. Day is over, it is nighttime now. . . .

Junk crossed the straggling fields and passed between two piles of bricks and stones and other stranger fragments.

Suddenly there was no more green, not so much as a single weed. The waste stretched out ahead, bleak and bare. In the distance there was a little group of jagged broken shapes, like dead trees on the horizon; but they must have been much taller than trees. Close at hand, the road they had followed from the second wagon-halt out of Mosden came out of another gap in the villagers' wall. It was now a broad gray ribbon, leading them away. The hard undersurface that had been buried in Inland was revealed. It looked smooth from a distance, though it was really pockmarked and broken. Junk slipped along between hummocks and hillocks that broke up the ground beside it, ready to take cover. There was no sign of life, but they were taking no chances.

Dimen heard Zanne whisper to herself, "the land of the towers of light. . . . " She grinned wryly. Imagination is a wonderful thing, she thought. But she didn't have the heart to tease; her friend's face was such a mixture of trouble and wonder. She's come to the land of her dreams, thought Dimen. And there's nothing here. Poor Zanne.

The ground ahead of them sloped downhill; it was possible to see quite a way. It wasn't long before Dimen noticed that there was more than one "ancient road." Zanne came to the first place where two gray tracks met. She didn't hesitate. The next crossing was more complicated; no road was going quite in their direction. Zanne chose the widest way, without saying a word.

"Zanne—"

"It's all right," she answered firmly. "I saw all this from my lift. I won't get lost. I'm heading for the Daymaker. I know it."

Dimen relapsed into silence. She could see by the set of Zanne's jaw that it was no use. She didn't want to quarrel. She wasn't feeling well. She had a headache again, and a muzzy feeling like the start of a fever. There was something

106

in this air that didn't agree with Inlanders. Weakly, she told herself that even Zanne must decide to turn back soon.

They had left the village in early afternoon, after several delays caused by people who wanted more magic; and others wanting more money. They halted at dark, opened their packs and discovered that some of the Townsend rations had vanished. This was outrageous. They had bought everything they ate in the village, using up all of Dimen's coin. But there was no remedy. Dimen wanted to reckon up how many days' food they had left. Zanne wouldn't let her. It was an uneasy night.

In the morning Junk carried them on. Soon after they started off, something rather frightening happened. They ran into a whirlpool in the air. The wind came from nowhere, slinging dust in their eyes and making Junk leap and buck like a wild pony. For a moment it seemed they had been engulfed in a wholesale dust storm: but then as suddenly the wind was gone. They looked back and saw dust whirling in a cloud as wide as a house and spinning upwards toward the dull clouds. After that Zanne tried to watch out for these eddies and avoid them. But they kept taking her by surprise. She was afraid Junk would break up under the strain. There was nothing for it but to get onto the road, where at least there would be a level surface under them.

Dimen made no comment as Zanne steered Junk over the track, like a giant snail trail, that she had chosen out of yesterday's maze. She quietly retired into the shelter.

The borderland had vanished over the horizon now. There was nothing but the road, and the dust eddies whirling over bare waste on either side. Zanne saw other places where haze patches stood: reaching from the clouds to the ground. They were quite still, but somehow threatening. She hoped Junk wouldn't meet one. Soon the road began to run between banks of earth. The banks grew until Junk was sailing along the floor of a canyon.

Zanne steered straight, between low, weird cliffs that slipped by at a fast walking pace. She was getting frightened. She had said she would know the Daymaker because it would be "like nothing else in the world." But there was nothing of her world left here. The vision that she had seen from the air haunted her. Was Inland really such a small, frail thing? But still she was mostly frightened that Dimen was going to make her turn back.

Dimen crawled out of the shelter. "I've just rationed the food," she announced ominously.

Zanne's mouth set in an obstinate line; she kept on looking straight ahead.

"We have to turn back," said Dimen. "We were never ready for a trip this long, and now those thieving villagers have made things even worse. I'm sorry, but there it is."

She tried hard to keep the relief out of her voice.

"No!"

"We go back or we starve."

"I'm going to find the Daymaker."

"Zanne, we've got no idea where it is, or even what it is. And you know very well we aren't following the right road anymore. Besides which, you can make this uncovenanted rubbish fly—but even you can't eat it. Be reasonable."

Tears started in Zanne's eyes: tears of rage because Dimen was right.

"I won't be called a Covenant breaker by anyone!"

"I didn't—!"

"You did—!"

They were engrossed in their anger, both standing in the high stern.

"Stop this thing!" yelled Dimen. "I'm going home if I have to walk!"

And then Junk did stop. It hung in the air. Zanne and Dimen, silenced, were staring at a shaft of metal that had just grown out of Junk's gunwale. It was flighted in metal too: the whole thing was blue-black, with a wicked glister.

There were five armed figures, standing in the canyon. The girls looked around. The same number were forming up behind, the last of them just clambering out from behind one of the rubble heaps that lined the base of the high banks here. One of them was the "zany" who had begged for white bread.

"I knew he was spying," said Zanne bitterly.

The raiders closed in, ambling slowly with broad, lazy grins. Chief among them seemed to be a woman of middling height, with clear pale eyes in a weatherbeaten face. She wore a leather cap that covered her hair, decorated jauntily with a skull done in mirror fragments of glass. Shiny jangles of red and silver and blue were stitched on the sleeves of her jacket, and around the tops of her boots.

Zanne knew she couldn't lift Junk, not far enough or fast enough to get away from crossbow bolts. She brought it to the ground instead, and quickly jumped out.

"New to the Outlands, ain't you, girls?" said the outlaw chief in a friendly tone. "Wher' you from?"

"We're from Fatland," answered Zanne cheerfully, standing between the raiders and Junk's square bow. Dimen, who had stayed in the stern, grinned at the others coming up behind, doing her best to look dangerous.

"Stringer," announced the outlaw, holding out a lean and dirty hand.

"Zanne of Garth," replied Zanne, taking it. A faint shock went through her, possibly of fear. She tried not to show anything in her face.

"And this is—?"

"Dimen of Mosden."

"Well—welcome home, Zanne and Dimen."

There was no doubt that they had been ambushed, on information given by the ungrateful borderer. But the purpose of the ambush seemed entirely friendly. Stringer didn't ask what they were doing out here. She said that they had better join her patrol. In fact, she invited them—in a burst of grinning generosity—to spend the night at Flying Road, her band's home camp.

"It's good to have company at night in the Outlands," said Stringer. "I don't want to scare you, but not every band's as harmless as mine. And there are the ghost patches, and the windpools. Bad to hit a windpool in the darkness. Or to have one hit you."

There was nothing to do but accept the offer gratefully and cheerfully, while wondering unhappily what was the real object.

"It can't be money," muttered Dimen. "Because that young brute already knows exactly what's in our packs."

"Perhaps they mean to hold us for ransom."

The outlaws had horses, which were brought out from behind the rubble when the greetings were over. Dimen noticed that they were well fed enough, though not particularly well groomed. Stringer left the girls to claim her mount. She came back with a squat grim looking man in black. He carried his crossbow on one arm still. It looked as if it grew there.

"This is Bolt," she announced. "My second. He'd like to ride with you."

Bolt said nothing. He ran his hand along Junk's side. He and Stringer looked at each other, thought Dimen, like people who have just bought something cheap, from a fool who doesn't know the proper price.

"He can't," said Zanne firmly. "Junk will only fly for me and Dimen."

110

Stringer was disappointed but she laughed and accepted that. However, when the party set off, Junk was in the middle. And the riders adapted to the pace of the craft, never letting it fall behind.

It was a long way back to camp. They didn't stay on Zanne's road but left it soon for another, even wider track, which had no banks but drove straight across the bare, dusty plain. Stringer stayed close beside Junk. Either because of her skill or because it recognized Covenant magic, her animal did not object to the weird object. She pointed out the sights—distant ruins where her band and others scavenged for metal and other useful material. She told them again how lucky they had been to meet her. Flying Road band didn't often venture so far from home.

"At least," she laughed, "not at this season, eh Fat-landers?"

When she left them briefly to consult with her second, Zanne took the chance to whisper to Dimen.

"What d'you think?"

Dimen was staring out at the wasteland. "Why is it so dead?" she muttered. "Nothing rots away, and yet nothing grows. . . . "

There was certainly a mystery. But at the moment Zanne was more interested in practical questions.

"What d'you think?" she asked again. "Are they really friendly?"

Dimen raised her eyebrows, with an expression that annoyed Zanne.

"Of course not."

Dusk came and a wind began to rise, keening across the empty darkening sky. The outlaws set a brisker pace. In their country, night was something to be feared.

At last, just before full dark, they came to Flying Road. It was the remains of a meeting of ancient ways, on a grander scale than anything Zanne and Dimen had yet seen. One road was lifted up on great piers, and now ended in space. Another went diving beneath; and between the two was a swooping knot of secondary ways, steeply banked or balanced on stilts. In the dusk, with the whitish piers gleaming, it looked like a battle of giant snakes, frozen in stone.

The outlaw patrol came down from the upper road, into a wide hollow under the snakes' bellies. There was a sprawling huddle of huts; some built of and half buried in heaps of rubble where bits of raised road had fallen. Right under the place where the big flying road broke off, a huge smoking wildfire had been lit. Outlaws emerged from the huts and got up from the fire. When they saw Zanne and Dimen and Junk they began to whoop and yell.

"I think we were expected," murmured Dimen.

Stringer took the girls to the fire, an arm around each of them.

"I've brought us some new recruits!" she announced. All the outlaws laughed, so Dimen and Zanne laughed too; it seemed better not to argue.

Zanne was not afraid. These people looked dirtier and shabbier than the raiders she had once met in Garth woods, but also less dangerous. She had been thinking as she rode along in their company, how unfair the Inlanders were to Outlanders. To Inland these were "the badlands," but to the outlaws Inland was Fatland. It was really quite silly. And no wonder they had to raid their neighbours, since nothing would grow out here. The coveners of Inland kept all their magic for their own land and gave Outsiders only a miserable dole of food. She felt excited now. She and Dimen had no reason to fear. They brought the gift of magic, as they had brought it to the border village.

Dimen knew Zanne was going to do something foolish.

She could see it in the dear turniphead's bright eyes. She tried her best to signal, but Stringer got between them.

Zanne smiled around her, fearlessly.

"You've heard, haven't you, what we did on the border? Don't worry—we'll help you too."

There was a man in front of her with a filthy bandage tied round his shoulder. Zanne reached out, to show her meaning. The man snarled like a beast. Something bright flashed instantly into his hand. Dimen gave a kind of moan....

Zanne looked at the knife, still completely without fear. She turned to Stringer.

"What did I do wrong?"

The raiders laughed.

"Don't be offended, girls," cried Stringer. "Your mumbo jumbo's not for us. That's all."

"Yeah. We know what you are."

"But that stuff's not for us."

"If we wanted Fatland ways, we'd live in Fatland."

Zanne began to protest. Dimen pinched her arm, shaking her head urgently. Before Zanne could find out what that was about, Stringer pounced again, squeezing Zanne's shoulder in one hand and Dimen's in the other.

"Come on and eat," she cried. "I'm hungry as a wolf!"

There was a supper served around the fire, of mutton and bread and beer. Zanne was in high spirits. It wasn't until she had taken her first bite of half-roasted meat and fat that the significance occurred to her. Then, at once, she was in Garth. She could see her mother, kneeling in somebody's barnyard, speaking the quiet words of covenanted death.

"Stringer," she asked sharply. "How do you kill your meat?"

The woman beside her grinned, and winked broadly.

"Mostly," she chuckled, "I use a knife."

113

It was a stupid question. Zanne went on eating, though her mouth was full of ashes and the greasy chopbone in her fingers suddenly weighed like lead. Uncovenanted flesh—it wasn't only wicked, it was poison. No wonder these outlaws and borderers looked so unhealthy. But she hardened her heart. When the Daymaker was found it would all be worthwhile.

Dimen ate a little, she didn't want to attract attention. But the food tasted foul to her. She was still feeling ill, and she now sensed the nature of this illness. It was not physical, it was worse than that. But she had to keep her head. Zanne was just too innocent to deal with these people.

"So what you want with us, Stringer?"

"Eh?"

The outlaw looked hurt.

"Come on now. You know and we know we didn't meet by accident. That lad from the village must've run like a hare straight to your patrol. And out you came to collect us. What do you want?"

Stringer laughed. She winked at Zanne confidentially.

"Darkie's a sharp one."

"Well—?" persisted Dimen, using the hard but good humored tone her mother used on gravel merchants.

Stringer looked wise. She sat up, the bone in her fingers stripped clean as a whistle by her efficient white teeth. She threw it on the fire and chuckled.

"It's like this, girls. You can't help us. But we can help you. You're looking for the Daymaker, aren't you? Well, we're the ones to take you to it."

She grinned triumphantly. Dimen was trying to look noncommittal, but it was a waste of time with Zanne there.

"Back at the border they said you were coming to turn the Daymaker on again. Is that true?"

"I'm going to try," said Zanne.

Stringer looked at her hard, as if something was confirmed.

"Good enough. Now, I know what you think of us in Fatland. But it's not the whole story. We reckon we're the loyal ones."

She nodded gravely.

"We remember the old times, see. That's why I said 'Welcome home, girls.' We want more from life than turnip growing. So we manage without that farmer-bumpkin magic, and we want for a lot of things you Fatlanders take for granted. But if you can fix the Daymaker, we won't want for anything. There's makers in the ruins out here, and metal to build more. We're not afraid of work. We'll trade the things the makers make, and we won't have to come raiding. Ain't that right, friends?"

The crowd of outlaws added their assent. A chorus of voices rose in a ragged cheer.

"The Daymaker! The Daymaker!"

Everything was all right again. Zanne looked at Dimen with stars in her eyes. And Dimen couldn't spoil the moment. She had to smile as well.

Bolt, the silent lieutenant, was stretched out on the ground on the other side of Zanne. He grinned and winked at his neighbors as the cheer died down.

"Nah—no more robbing. Stringer 'ates robbing."

"Shut up, Bolt."

She turned back to Zanne and Dimen with an easy smile.

"You noticed what I said to you? I said 'welcome home'—"

"So where is the Daymaker?" broke in Dimen. "How long will it take to get there?"

For a moment Stringer showed a different face. The teeth stayed but the smile vanished. Then she laughed.

"Ah—quiet down, Darkie. Give us a chance."

115

She jumped to her feet, stretching her arms and yawning. "It'll wait till morning, wherever it is."

The girls slept in Junk. This was not Stringer's idea. She was worried for them; sleeping out of doors was not safe. But she gave way, after making sure the magic boat was brought close to the big central fire, into an alley between two rows of huts.

It was cramped inside the shelter, but they were getting used to that, and both of them were glad of a chance to speak freely.

"Lucky they didn't accept your offer of magic," remarked Dimen grimly.

"Why do you say that? I wanted to help—"

"Because it might not have worked, and then we'd have been in trouble. Look at that."

Dimen's moonlamp was standing on top of their packs, lighting the shelter with a dim yellow glow like a single candle.

"The outlaws are right. Covenant magic lives in the natural world. And in the 'minds and hearts,' you know. There is no Covenant here. I can certainly feel the difference. Can't you?"

The moon flame wavered uncertainly.

Zanne was silent for a moment. She had thought Dimen was keeping the light low on purpose.

"Er—I suppose so."

She woke in the night. Lying with her eyes open she saw only charcoal-colored darkness, but felt the contours of her pack and heard Dimen's breathing. Junk was not fixed to the ground. It moved a little, as if rocked by a distant wind. But there was no sound from outside. Zanne had the strange thought that there was nothing out there, only a wind-rocked grayness, going on forever. She thought of the wasteland as she had seen it from above—like a great lake with no farther shore. Now she was floating in that emptiness. The raiders and their camp, the snake roads and distant ruins—none of it existed. Her face was cold. Still, there was nothing unnatural in that. You could be chilly at Midsummer anywhere in Inland.

She reached out and touched Junk's side. This craft was made of neither wood nor stone, nor metal out of the rock. But it answered Zanne. Dimen was wrong. There was still magic here.

"There *is* a Covenant between me and you," she whispered. "Don't listen to them, Junk. I love you just as much as if you were made of flowers."

Then she slept, reassured. But Dimen tossed and turned as if she was in a fever, and she had bad dreams.

The outlaws of Flying Road were not early risers. They emerged slowly, scratching themselves, lounging about, kicking at the ashes of the fire. Some started to prepare food, some settled to bone dice or wandered off to workplaces in the camp, which was really a small town. Zanne and Dimen waited for hours before Zanne finally admitted the truth. There was no plan to set off for the great Maker today. She asked then for directions, so that they could go on alone. But Stringer explained, very reasonably, that she couldn't allow that. The Outland was too dangerous.

"And be fair, girls. We found you. We've got a right to our share. I'll take you—maybe tomorrow."

There were between thirty and forty people living at Flying Road. Some were no older than Zanne, but there were no children. Outlaw children were brought up in the border villages because infants sickened and died in the Outland: no one knew why.

When not occupied in raiding Inland, Flying Road's people spent their time feuding with other bands, scavenging the wasteland and making weapons and other necessaries out of their haul. Zanne and Dimen saw horse-drawn sleds coming in, loaded with strange refuse. The metal was melted down in a wildfire furnace. A variety of nameless rubbish went into what was known as "the still" and was boiled up to produce eventually a liquid that Stringer called lamp oil. It was a kind of raw spirit; some of the outlaws even drank it. A pall of evil-smelling smoke hung over the settlement all day, continually dispersed by the roving winds and continually reforming. It was no wonder, Dimen remarked, that the babies died here.

The raiders were very friendly to Darkie and Yellowhead. The ones who could speak Inland's language plainly told stories to entertain their guests—of murder and brutality among the feuding bands, of what Stringer did to those who crossed her, of the interesting effect when you poured lamp-oil over an enemy and set it alight. They reminisced about the raiding season, when turnip-magic was half asleep and it was possible to break in and strip a fat town or two, and hunt deer in the forest. The two-legged kind, they said, gave the best sport. They had a sinister way of talking as if Darkie and Yellowhead were not guests at all, but part of the family. It didn't matter that they had come from Inland. That inconvenience could soon be forgotten—as some of Flying Road's people had reason to know.

Zanne returned friendliness with friendliness, and tried not to flinch even from the worst stories. She pitied these poor people; she didn't blame them. Dimen was very quiet.

So that day passed, and another. On the third day Zanne woke with renewed hope, to find Dimen sitting opposite staring at her moonlamp. It was dull and dead. As soon as she saw that her friend was awake, Dimen quickly put the lamp away. But Zanne had seen her face.

"Dimen, what's wrong?"

"Nothing," said Dimen: then she changed her mind. She sighed heavily. "My magic has gone."

Zanne was horrified. She found the pebble from Hillen moor, and it was soon proved that her talent was still untouched by this mysterious sickness.

"We'd better go back at once," she said quickly. "You were all right until we left Inland."

Dimen was touched. She knew how much it would cost Zanne to give up her precious Daymaker. But she shook her head. Dimen had been thinking hard, these past two days.

"It's not so easy, Zanne. These outlaws expect you to turn on the Daymaker. Whatever that means. They might get nasty if we try to leave now. We'll have to humor them—we need food and water. There's nothing to do but wait."

Dimen thought the Daymaker was probably a useless old heap of metal like the ones Zanne had described in the cave at Garth—if it existed at all. The legend of its fantastic powers was just wishful thinking. And Stringer didn't know where it was; she was just boasting. What Dimen really hoped was that Stringer wouldn't want to have her bluff called. In a few days she would be happy to let "Darkie and Yellowhead" go on their way.

She didn't tell Zanne this. She still didn't want to be the one to spoil her friend's adventure.

But then something happened that changed both of their ideas about the jolly rogues of Flying Road.

The raiders had no true magic. It seemed that apart from Zanne's power, true magic could not exist in Outland. Everyone at Flying Road was very impressed by Junk. But quite a few of them, it turned out, had the same sort of talent as Zanne's Uncle Lol. These "illusion-merchants" were always playing tricks on the rest. It was a great joke to fool someone into trying to bite a stone or a greasy rag in mistake for meat or bread, or to have your victim walk into the fire.

Stringer was the worst of the lot. She would sit and watch one of her people cleaning a weapon, and stare until the unlucky one was forced to throw the parts away, or stick them in the fire and pull them out again—red hot. It was obvious that her skill in this kind of magic had earned her her command. The outlaws said admiringly that "she could make you eat your own hand."

The Inland girls were both disgusted by all this. But, Zanne argued, people couldn't help being nasty when they lived in such a horrible place.

On the afternoon of their third day at Flying Road, the camp was very quiet. Everyone seemed to have disappeared. Dimen went to fill the waterbottles at a brackish spring under one of the stilt roads. That was the only source of water.

Zanne stayed with Junk. She had put a warding on the craft so it should be safe from interference, but Dimen insisted one of them always had to be near it. She was alone except for three raider girls, who sat gossiping at the door of a nearby hut. She saw Dimen coming back, and knew before the other girl spoke that there was something very wrong.

"Shall we go for a walk?" said Dimen, in a loud and artificially natural voice.

She led the way, up to the flying road. The three young raiders followed. They stopped where the broken road bridge launched itself into space: the two "recruits" weren't going very far that way.

"What is it, Dimen? Why the mystery?"

"Look."

Zanne looked. Beyond the huts on the lower level, there were the barns full of horse feed, stolen from Inland and from the border villagers. In between, beside the horse corral, there was a rough square of well-trodden dirt. Nearly the whole population of Flying Road was gathered there, sitting on the ground. Stringer was sitting out on her own in front of them. Between her and the rest two raiders stood, holding a third between them.

"It looks like a Covenant meeting!" exclaimed Zanne.

"That's what I thought. Now watch what happens."

They watched, and soon they would have liked to stop watching, but they couldn't tear their eyes away. At a sign from the Stringer the two who were obviously guards stood back. The chief took a knife from her belt. She put the point to her teeth and bit at it reflectively. She laughed—Dimen and Zanne heard that clearly—and tossed it so it landed at the prisoner's feet. The woman bent down stiffly, and picked it up. Then, horribly, she seemed to try and throw it away. But the knife stayed in her hand. Like a live, separate thing the hand twisted the knife around. . . .

Zanne gasped and hid her face; so did Dimen.

When they looked again, Stringer was sitting as before. Between her and the ground, there was a whirling column of dust. As the girls watched, it rose and flowed away. A woman's body lay on the ground. The shadow of her death drifted and spread—dropping on the raiders' faces, dropping on the land all around Flying Road. And further still, becoming one with the waste.

"I didn't mean you to see that," whispered Dimen. "It wasn't so bad when I passed. Must've been lesser crimes."

They had known that the outlaws were murderers. It was different to see it happen. And there was something here worse than murder.

"Zanne," said Dimen steadily. "I know what happens at a Covenant meeting. The covener brings the minds of the people together. And their needs and her magic work on the world. To shift it or hold it. But what did this meeting do to this world?"

The raider girls were still watching. They were grinning

121

and nudging each other, pleased that the strangers had had a good fright.

"Inland is made of magic," said Zanne softly.

She had been told that often, and thought she understood. She had been just a child reciting a lesson. She had never really known, until this journey, how strange it was to live in a world of magic. And how dangerous it might be.

"Tecov Pompe says, remember: 'If you look very closely at anything, all that seems fixed and definite dissolves.' "

"I remember that. I thought it was a joke—the disappearing tables and chairs."

"It's not a joke. At the essential level, we make the world ourselves every moment, out of our intentions and desires. That is how magic operates. Outland is made of magic too. That's what we didn't know. And we have just seen the kind of magic that makes it."

"I knew there was nothing natural about this dead waste," muttered Dimen. "Your outlaws aren't forced to live in a dust bowl, Zanne. This place is exactly the way they want it to be. It won't change, until they change first."

Suddenly Zanne grasped her friend's hand. Her eyes were full of horror.

"Oh, Dimen, you are better than me. Your magic is gone because you don't want Outland to be like this. But I—"

"Oh no—" cried Dimen. "You're not like them. You just have a very strong talent. Everybody says so."

They had been talking in whispers, but their voices were raised now. They remembered, together, the raider girls. Zanne dropped Dimen's hand.

"Let's go back," she said out loud. But as they went calmly down the path she muttered under her breath. "We've got to get away, Dimen. We can't stay here now. Not even for the Daymaker."

Dimen felt the same. A few days of very short rations

seemed a small price to pay to escape from this unpleasant company.

Dimen had already discovered that Junk was watched at night. She told Zanne this, and found her now quite willing to believe that the "friendly" outlaws were dangerous. They must escape secretly. They both managed to smuggle bread away from the meal around the wildfire. In the early morning, Zanne went to the camp latrine wrapped in Dimen's wagon cloak against the chill. She had one pack under the cloak, holding all their useful rations and her own wagon cloak. She left it hidden on the path to the spring.

Junk would have to stay behind. They couldn't pretend to be going for a stroll if they took the magic boat along. Their plan was to leave it where it lay, with a coat and a pack clearly visible on the deck. Zanne would release the pattern and return Junk to its elements, as soon as the two of them were safely away. She didn't want any chance of the robbers misusing her magic. It hurt her to leave poor Junk. But there was no other way.

They decided at noon that their chance had come. The outlaws had been up late celebrating their "Covenant meeting." The camp was half asleep; neither Bolt nor Stringer had emerged. Zanne and Dimen set out to fill their water bottles, trusting no one would remember that Dimen had filled them yesterday.

They used none of Zanne's power for this escape. After what they had seen, it seemed as if any magic worked here would be infected with evil.

But the plan was not a clever one. It deserved to fail, and it did. Stringer's guards caught them, leading two of Flying Road's horses up a narrow track beside the spring. They were marched back to camp, without any pretense of friendliness.

Stringer was angry then. She stamped up and down in

front of her hut, scolding at them indignantly. She didn't expect disobedience from her recruits.

"But we're not—"

"Shut up, Yellowhead. I'm the chief here. I say what you are. And horse-thieves too. I ought to make you hang yourselves!"

The skull on Stringer's cap winked unpleasantly. She bit her thumb and glared.

"I've been too nice to you, that's what it is. I'm *protecting* you. You don't know you're alive, little girls. If you were to meet my chief, you'd soon wish you were back with Stringer."

The punishment for horse stealing and attempted desertion was a night in the lockup. Under the piers of one of the raised roads was a row of bunkers used for storage. Zanne and Dimen were thrust into one of these, a crude but secure metal door slammed and bolted behind them. The bunker had recently been used for storing meat carcasses. There were hooks in the roof, and the floor was greasy and noisome. The air stank.

They crouched in the evil-smelling dark, on a small patch of relatively clean floor. The pack and water bottles had been confiscated. Before they were locked in, they had been forced to strip and given tattered leather breeches and jackets in place of their own clothes. Stringer said it was time they learned to give up Fatland ways. When they were caught, Zanne had managed to slip her moonlamp into her pocket: but now even that was gone.

"Well," said Dimen wryly, "it's nice to have things out in the open."

Zanne groaned and buried her head in her hands.

"I'm sorry, I'm sorry."

"It wasn't your fault. We were ambushed, remember."

"It's my fault we ever left Inland. It was all my idea. They

124

were never going to take us to the Daymaker. They don't know anything about it."

Dimen sighed in the darkness.

"I'm afraid not. I think they just liked the sound of the word."

"Like me," agreed Zanne, abjectly. "Oh, Dimen, I'm so sorry. For all of this."

Light came into the lock up through a fingernail crack at the lower edge of the door. But the bolt and hinges were out of reach and there was a guard outside. Groping examination proved the cave had not been made by the raiders. It was ancient work. Its corners were square; there were no cracks, no tunnels.

At last they tired of this examination. Zanne was wishing they had stopped to think. They might have managed to get away, with more care. But they had both been too shocked by Stringer's horrible abuse of magic.

Maybe Inland and Outland both were once dead waste, thought Zanne. After the land of the towers of light died. But Inland people made the Covenant, and the ruins changed to green fields. That's what death means. It means changing into something else. Outland had not died properly, that's what is wrong with it....

It was a distraction, to think; but even Zanne couldn't concentrate for long in this stinking prison. Soon she was only staring miserably. And the Daymaker, the Daymaker was just a grandpa's tale. It was all for nothing.

"We've got to escape tonight," said Dimen.

Zanne started. Dimen's words had broken a long silence.

"What do you mean?" she asked stupidly. "How can we?"

"By magic, of course."

There was a long pause.

"I can't do it," whispered Zanne.

"Zanne, I know how you feel. But we have to escape, and quickly. Really, we've been prisoners all along. But now we know it, and Stringer doesn't have to be polite and charming any more."

Zanne groaned.

Dimen groped for her hand. She felt she was being cruel, but she couldn't help it.

"You're special, Yellowhead. You can work true magic out here, with material things. Remember how Stringer and Bolt looked, when they first met Junk? Do you want to wait until they start *persuading* you to work for them?"

They couldn't see each other's faces. But at last Zanne laughed shakily.

"All right. Just tell me what to do and I'll do it."

"That'll make a change, my dear turniphead. We'll do nothing yet. Wait until it's dark outside."

They waited through the long slow hours of daylight. Night was their friend, after all. The raiders were afraid of the dark. Occasionally the line of light was blocked: the crunching footsteps of their guard shifted to and fro.

Stringer did not attempt to use her ugly power against the Hillen girls. Or perhaps she did. About dusk, the wind began to rise as usual. But it went on rising into a real battle, until the town was full of dust and flying refuse. The raiders were used to storms. But this one was unusually fierce. They kept undercover. No one lit the big fire. Only the guard in front of the lockup stayed out of doors, too terrified of Stringer to leave that post.

In total darkness Zanne ripped two fragments off the cuffs of her outlaw jacket. The leather was so worn it tore like paper. She dipped a finger in the grease on the floor and wrote on one piece D, on the other Z. Carefully she inserted first "Dimen" and then "Zanne" into the crack under the door, and the wind whipped them away into the howling night. It made her feel worse to use illusion tricks, just like the outlaws. But though she might have the power to break down the door, or transport herself and Dimen bodily out of the bunker, she didn't know how to set about it. She was only an apprentice still.

The prisoners heard their guard start up with a yell. In another moment the door was flung open. The flame of a lamp crackled and whipped about, its smoke stinging the girls' eyes. But the guard saw only an empty cell.

Dimen and Zanne stood against the wall, listening to the thump of their two hearts, and their thunderous breath. The tension was almost unbearable. They must not move.

But if he guessed what they had done, and got into the cell and shut the door, and started groping for their invisible bodies....

He did not. He charged off, shouting.

"They're out! They're out! The Fatlanders are getting away!"

A tumult rose: first Stringer's voice then others, fighting with the wind. Zanne put both her hands in a puddle of grease and smeared it over her hair, which was already dull and lank with dirt. Then she and Dimen ran, keeping to the shadow of the bunkers, dodging around the back of the furnace house. Raiders were rushing out of their hovels, with muttonfat torches and spirit lamps. Light splashed and vanished, flaming on savage faces. No laughing now, no mockery of friendship....

They found themselves together, backed up against the wall of the still. They could hear Stringer yelling directions. Between them and Junk was the wildfire circle, a churning mass of bodies and torches.

"Make us invisible again!" gasped Dimen.

"I can't! There are too many of them. And I'm too frightened!"

Stringer's voice came clearly.

"Get around the outside of the camp! Get out in a circle and beat in!"

Dimen started away, wildly lunging for the outer darkness. But Zanne grabbed her by the arm.

"No!"

She had suddenly realized they had only one good chance: to plunge through the middle of the camp.

"Outlaws!" she cried. "We're outlaws!"

It was true. In their filthy leathers, in the dark, they smelled like outlaws, felt like outlaws. There was not a trace left of the two Hillen students.

Dimen lost Zanne almost at once. She dodged and ducked in a nightmare confusion, and ran full tilt into a bulky shadow; fell on her face and came up clutching something in her fist. Her hand had fallen on a knife someone had dropped. She slashed out desperately—but her assailant was gone. She saw Junk: that unmistakable strange silhouette. There was someone there before her. With a gasp of relief she realized it was Zanne, her face striped with dirt and torchlight. She was tugging frantically at something Dimen couldn't see.

"They've tied it down! They've tied Junk down!"

Junk tried to fly and could not. It struggled like a fish in a net. The thongs were warped across its bows and again in front of the high stern, and fastened to lumps of rubble. Zanne heaved at the stones. She was in such a state of panic she could not reach her Link power: she could not move them.

Dimen leapt into the stern. She heard someone yelling in the hubbub behind them:

"Who's guarding that flying boat?" Sobbing in desperation, she flung herself at the leather, hacking with her outlaw knife.

"Get on board, Zanne. Get on board!"

The thongs parted; Zanne felt Junk slipping. She grabbed the side and rolled over it as the craft suddenly heaved itself free and shot backward.

Blood thundered in her ears. She could see faces, smell the smoke of lamp oil. She knelt and called on the storm, hardly knowing what she was doing or how much of the wild uproar was in her mind and how much outside.

Junk leapt. The faces were rushing up before it, and Zanne cried out in terror. All of Flying Road seemed to be howling together, like a pack of wolves. The wind had turned into a wolf too—a black wolf with a red mouth opening like a whirlpool; and the torches and the faces and glints of blue-black metal were all racing into that red pit, dragging Zanne and Dimen with them....

But it was Junk that was racing, speeding down the lower road in the darkness. Everything else had gone. Zanne saw the flare of torches falling away behind. And then it had vanished.

She clambered stiffly through the shelter. Silently, she took the steering oar from Dimen. Dimen crawled inside. There was no point in trying to talk, the wind howled so. After that it was better. Junk steadied. It knew Zanne's hand. She licked warm salt from her upper lip; she had smacked her nose falling onto the bottom boards and it was bleeding.

She felt sure there would be no pursuit from Flying Road. Not until morning anyway. But the knowledge did not comfort her. She was as bad as the raiders now. She had used tainted magic to cover their escape. She too was responsible for the dust and waste and misery of Outland.

The wind did not drop, but the buffets and side gusts were less violent after a while. The road was between high piles of rubble; black walls topped by a charcoal-gray sky. She saw a gap and guided Junk out onto the waste. Night seemed to welcome her. Perhaps it was just that out of the funnel of the road's banks, the storm was less. Like a good beast Junk seemed to find its own way to a place where two indistinct hummocks close together made a kind of shelter. Zanne let the craft come to rest. She wiped her nose on her foul-smelling leather sleeve and crawled into the shelter.

"I think we should stay here until morning."

"Where are we?"

"I don't know," said Zanne heavily.

Dimen's eyes and teeth smiled in the murk. Her arms came out of the ark and tucked a fold of warmth around Zanne's shoulders.

"Cheer up, little covenanter. Look what I found. My wagon cloak. And my pack's here too."

In the pack they found the remains of Dimen's collection of delicacies. Wrapped in one cloak they ate half a jar of wizened preserved peaches. Unfortunately Zanne had had the syrup from them after her long lift; it seemed like months ago. But there was moisture in the fruit. They chewed carefully. The sugar gave a much needed lift to their spirits.

"What are we going to do about water?" asked Zanne.

"Find some," answered Dimen firmly.

They were lost, and they would be hunted. Both of them remembered Stringer's warning. They could well believe there were monsters in this wasteland, even worse than they had yet seen. But they still had Junk, and a little food. Things were better than they might be.

So they told each other, and resolved to try and sleep. About an hour later, another storm found them. Zanne and Dimen didn't know it, but they had been blown straight to the center of that part of Outland where great windpools raced up and down devouring each other endlessly. Once this place had been a real physical focus of power, an ever hungry vortex, and nobody felt those winds. But that was in another age. This was Inland's time, and the storm was real.

It picked up Junk from the lee, without more than a second's howling warning. Zanne was flung into the stern with a violence that almost knocked her unconscious. Yelling at each other unintelligibly, they grabbed any hold they could find. The pack smacked Dimen in the jaw. She screamed and tried to snatch it, but the strap whipped through her fingers and was gone. The cloak wrapped itself around Zanne's legs, doing its best to drag her overboard. They were moving at a terrifying speed. For a freak moment Dimen heard what the voice in her ear was screaming.

"Jump clear! Jump clear!"

A great shape loomed up. There was an almighty crash.

Zanne crawled to her knees. She was holding something in one hand. It was part of Junk's steering oar.

"Are you all right?" she asked the gray darkness.

"Y-yes," came a shaky reply.

Zanne began to sob, hugging the bent pipe.

"Junk's dead. Poor brave Junk. It's dead!"

They were in the dark. Then miraculously, they were in the light. The change was so sudden that for a moment Zanne thought she had gone blind. She heard Dimen cry out. She found she was standing on a huge broad step, like the plinth under a statue but huge; stretching out in both directions. She could see this step because above it a door had opened: a small, human-size door in a blank black wall. Light came from within, and in the light was standing a young man, dressed for a feastday. He carried a lamp; the glow of it shone on his red gold hair. He was using his free hand to separate Dimen from her knife.

"Who are you?" cried Dimen again.

"I am Chiro," said the young man, and his fine robe flowed and rattled in the wind.

"Come inside. Come out of the storm. You are safe now."

# CHAPTER 7

THE DOOR WAS shut. They stood in a huge room, brightly lit with lamps and candles, the flames redoubled by their reflections in pale shining pavement and walls. Zanne and Dimen had seen intact piles of masonry around Flying Road, standing up like isolated crags in the distance. This must be one of those blocks. But there was no sign of ruin here, or dirt or decay. The man with red gold hair smiled at them. He wore a dark red open robe over brown velvet breeches and a spotless white shirt. There was a gold chain at his throat and a golden ring on his finger. He looked like the favored son of rich tradesfolk, dressed in his best to go to meeting.

"Who are you?" asked Dimen again.

"I am Chiro," he repeated, patiently. "I am the master here, with the lady Vanan. You are welcome to our house."

He grinned at their bewildered faces.

"Didn't you know? Weren't you trying to reach us? Well—perhaps you were and didn't know it. You've been very lucky anyway. A storm like that can kill, and our home is the only shelter you could have found. No ghost winds get through our walls!"

Zanne and Dimen looked at each other in blank amazement.

"This is your *home*?" repeated Dimen, staring at the shining walls. "What kind of place is this?"

Zanne could still hear the frustrated whining of the storm. But it sounded impossibly small and far away. They had walked through a door, and the whole world had changed.

Chiro started to laugh. It was a friendly human sound. It brought them back to their senses, partly.

"Don't be afraid," he soothed them. "Don't worry about anything. Vanan will explain."

He clapped his hands twice.

Two women appeared, dressed soberly and carrying lamps. They could have popped out of slots in the floor, for all Zanne and Dimen could make out. Their faces were as blank as if they really were toys.

Zanne hardly knew what was happening. She found herself walking up to a curved stairway and into a dim room, that became bright as the toy women lit lamps that hung from brackets on the walls. Inside an inner door there was a bath standing on tiles. Zanne, quite dazed, let the women help her out of her clothes while a whole procession of plain-clad silent people arrived with coppers full of steaming hot water.

"You bathe," said the first woman in a flat churlish tone. "Lady Vanan wants."

So she bathed, wondering vaguely what had happened to Dimen. Had she vanished forever, the way people do in dreams? But it was so wonderful to wash off the layers of grime, that even Dimen seemed less important. She dried herself on the linen towels that lay waiting and rubbed her clean hair to yellow fluff. The woman had taken away her filthy leathers. In the outer room, she found that a bed had been made up, and a rug spread on the floor. There were clean clothes laid out on the coverlet; underwear and tunic and leggings as fine as anything you could find in Mid Inland. They did not fit well, and were a little fusty as if taken out of long storage. But the change was still delightful.

She went out of her room and almost immediately the next door opened. There was Dimen, dressed in blue and green velvet, her long black hair loose and glistening. They stared at each other, silenced by astonishment.

Chiro was watching from the hall below.

"We're waiting for you," he called. "Come and eat."

Under the gallery a pair of tall doors stood open, leading into another room as large as the first, with beautiful woven hangings covering the lower walls. A table was set for four at the far end. As Chiro led the two girls in, a woman rose from behind this table and came toward them. She was as well-dressed as the young man, but more plainly. She had a broad, pale-skinned face, not handsome but with deep and intelligent dark eyes. She walked forward until she stood in front of Zanne, and looked into her face with an extraordinarily penetrating expression.

"So this is 'Yellowhead,'" she said at last. "Welcome, my child. I have been waiting for you for a long, long time."

Zanne started back, suddenly wary. It was the raiders who had called her Yellowhead.

Vanan laughed a little.

"Oh yes. I make it my business to know what goes on out there, even though I cannot always control the bands. You're safe from Stringer now. The ruffians of Flying Road will not follow you here."

"We will explain everything," broke in Chiro. "But let's eat first. You must be sick for the sight of good food if you have been trying to live on the muck the bands eat."

The dinner was of preserved meats and fruits, and white bread. It was very grand. More of the soberly dressed people waited at table. Zanne had realized by now they were servants, like the ones she'd met at Dimen's house. She was glad of her visits to the Roadkeepers; otherwise she would not have known how to be waited on. Or how to manage the cutlery and napery. Chiro and Vanan both drank wine. The guests refused, and were served water flavored with lemon or rose from two exquisite crystal jugs.

It was very like being in Oldmarket Street in fact, because Vanan asked questions just like Dimen's mother. Not about the outlaws, or how Dimen and Zanne came to be here, but about Hillen, and other Inland affairs. She seemed very knowledgeable. They answered politely. Vanan's voice and manner had authority, kindly but not to be resisted.

That young man's a bit of a fool, thought Dimen. But this is an important person. She's like our town covener. How does she come to be living alone out here?

At last the table was cleared.

"Now then," said Vanan. "We can speak freely. My servants don't listen to what I don't want them to hear. Still, it is better not to take risks."

But something had happened to Zanne, as the last silent figure disappeared. She woke up. She finally realized what a strange place this was. She looked around her wildly.

"Where does all this come from?" she cried. "I can't believe it. How can there be a house like this in Outland? It's grander than anything I've ever seen. It's like the land of the towers of light!"

Chiro laughed out loud.

"Oh no," Vanan smiled. "We are not ghosts. Everything you see is real. I am a student of the past, Zanne. That is why I make my home here, in what you Inlanders call a barren waste. But believe me, there is more to be found in the badlands than you were ever taught at Hillen. There are other great houses like this, and vaults full of treasure, sealed against time. Perhaps the coveners are not anxious for the truth to be known. They would have all their young people running away to make their fortunes—instead of just a venturesome few."

She smiled at the girls. Zanne smiled back, acknowledging the compliment. Dimen was still too wary for that.

Vanan leaned forward over the table, suddenly serious.

"Zanne of Garth and Dimen of Mosden," she remarked. "That's better. I mustn't go on calling you Yellowhead and Darkie. True names are important."

Zanne frowned. The penetrating, almost hungry look had come back to Vanan's eyes, and she didn't like it. But she forgot her unease immediately, at the woman's next words.

"You have come looking for the Daymaker, I understand."

Both girls stiffened. Dimen half got to her feet, as if the dignified lady had threatened to attack them. She sat down again, confused. Vanan was only nodding calmly.

"Don't be startled. As I explained, I gather information. We have to know what the bands are doing; it's the only way we can live safely. I am not Stringer. Believe me. *I know where the great Maker is. I can lead you to it.* But I am not going to bully you. I will tell you all I know, and then you will make up your own mind whether you want to go on with your quest."

She paused, thoughtfully.

"This is our problem, in the Outland. We believe that if the Daymaker was functioning it would produce its own power, by means unknown in our present world. But we need great power of some kind to begin that process. Until the Daymaker is functioning, there is no power in the world but magic. And true magic, as you will know by now, does not survive outside the borders of Inland. So you see, you are a very remarkable person, Zanne. Now you understand why I said I have been waiting for you for a long time."

Zanne stared, as if mesmerized.

Chiro turned to her eagerly.

"We heard of you and your flying boat. Vanan knew at

once that meant true magic. We've never had such a chance before. We were getting ready to come after you, when you turned up on your own. Stringer's a greedy fool. She doesn't know anything—"

Vanan frowned at him.

But Zanne wasn't listening to Chiro.

"Why shouldn't I want to carry on with my quest?" she asked slowly.

"Because the Daymaker is guarded, Zanne. Hillen Coven guards it, even at this distance. It seems they cannot destroy a great Maker. But they can keep the doors barred, at least against a mere scholar. You see, Zanne, your teachers are determined that the towers of light will never be rebuilt. You will have to defy them. Are you brave enough?"

Dimen said suddenly. "But, Zanne, I thought we agreed. We were going to forget about the Daymaker. We were going home."

Zanne looked at her in indignant surprise.

"Enough," said Vanan quickly. "You are both very tired, and I am being impatient. It will be a while before this storm blows itself out, and we can arrange to send you safely home. If that is what you want. You will have plenty of time, Zanne, to decide what you ought to do."

In the days that followed, the visitors didn't see much of Vanan. Chiro said she spent most of her time studying and didn't like to be disturbed. When they all four met at meals she always talked to Zanne, and soon discovered the whole story of her love for the makers. She herself had exciting plans for the future, if ever they could be carried out. She knew where there were rooms and rooms like the vault Zanne had found by the Moss. How rich Outland would be, and how wonderful it would be to see the beautiful metal beasts work and sing. . . .

138

When Vanan disappeared, Chiro was always available. He was there whenever Zanne and Dimen left their rooms, dismissing the taciturn servants when he saw they made Zanne uncomfortable. Outside the storm still raged, but he kept them amused. He showed them around the great house; as much of the building, that is, as he could show. There were doors that had been sealed for hundreds of years, rooms that no one had entered since the time of the towers of light.

Chiro did his best to be friendly to both his guests but he was obviously drawn to Zanne. She often surprised his light, clear hazel eyes watching her with admiration, and then Chiro would smile a little ruefully and turn away. Zanne was flattered. Dimen was supposed to be the good-looking one. And Chiro's interest was pleasantly mingled with real respect. Zanne's magic must be very strong, he said, to survive out here. Zanne must be very wise to have such power and skill at such a young age. Chiro couldn't claim any knowledge for himself. He could not even read. The books that lay about in chests, in careless display, were no more to him—he confessed with a laugh—than so much currency. Just as they might be to any miserable raider.

At Flying Road, Zanne had almost come to hate her own impervious magic. Surely any good and natural talent should have died, as Dimen's talent had died, in this unnatural land. It was a great relief to listen to Vanan and Chiro, and feel self-confidence return.

She had been simply bewildered at first, by this extraordinary change of fortune. And almost angry with Vanan. The search for the Daymaker had been Zanne's private adventure. Now suddenly everyone seemed to know about it—even the Tecovs at Hillen. But the anger wore off. Vanan made her feel special and brave.

She spoke very wisely about the outlaws too. Some people are born so, said the scholar. They find a rigid rule like the

Covenant too confining. They need to be free. Zanne listened, and knew Vanan was talking about herself as well as the outlaws. She felt that she too must be one of these superior people. She put out of her mind the ugly things she had learned at Flying Road. The bands would give up their unpleasant ways when they had makers to work for them. They wouldn't raid Inland any more, either.

It was easier to forget about Stringer, that evil covener of a lost meeting, because Vanan rarely mentioned "magic" at all. She didn't ask for any proof of Zanne's power. She gave the impression that all magic was almost beneath her notice, far inferior to the power the Daymaker would produce. And Zanne was quite ready to agree.

She was not afraid, either, to defy Hillen Coven. She had known she was doing that, after all, when she first started out. The only problem was Dimen. She would not approve. She wanted to go home. She did not trust Vanan and Chiro; she was sure they were "up to no good."

They argued in whispers at night. A servant slept in the slip of a room between their two chambers—this was part of the rich and ceremonial manner of life in Vanan's house.

"You notice she's not going to take you to the Daymaker until you first agree to turn against Hillen."

"It isn't like that," explained Zanne patiently. "I'm not turning against anything. I'm just making up my own mind. I'm entitled to do that, under the Covenant."

"I trust Hillen Coven. If they have this thing locked up, there is probably a very good reason."

Zanne was not convinced. She thought Dimen was being spineless. And often Dimen couldn't even convince herself. Whenever Vanan was present, dignified and kind, it was very hard to believe she was lying. But always Dimen's uneasiness started up again. Especially at night when Zanne had gone to sleep. Then the great strange house seemed to surround her with a hungry, watching presence. If she slept at all she dreamed she was back at Flying Road, in that foul-smelling prison with a guard outside the door.

In the evenings after Vanan returned to her studies the three younger people would sit in a blaze of candles and spirit lamps. Towers of light grew from the shining pavement as Zanne made visible her dream land of the past—and perhaps the future. Chiro was entranced. But Dimen stared at nothing, hardly uttering a word. Zanne was embarrassed for her, and did her best to cover her friend's rudeness.

Behind the two big front rooms, the offices of the castle began: the kitchen, the stores, the servants' quarters. Beyond these and down a flight of stone steps was a covered courtyard of sizable dimensions. It had been turned into a stable, with stalls built neatly between the smooth ancient pillars that held up the roof. Chiro brought his guests to see the horses. There were only a few animals in the rows of stalls.

"Our people go out regularly," he explained. "To keep an eye on the bands."

A servant came and called Chiro away. There was only one groom in sight; she moved closer when Chiro was gone, and stayed idling within earshot.

"I hate these servants," said Dimen suddenly, under her breath.

Zanne raised her eyebrows.

"I don't see why. You have plenty of them at your house."

Dimen's eyes flashed. "If you can compare my parents' staff to these dumb slaves—"

"Well, what—?"

The older girl shook her head. "Nothing, Zanne." The groom slouched away. "They never leave us alone," she added softly.

"Oh don't be stupid. When is anyone ever 'alone' at Hillen? Or at your house either."

Dimen was staring at the outer gates. They were very old, though not as old as the block itself, and barred with a massive beam of metal. It looked immovable.

"It's a pity we didn't meet Vanan's people," remarked Zanne. "Instead of Stringer's band."

"Maybe we did."

"Dimen? What do you mean?"

"Maybe we did meet Vanan's people. Chiro and she seem to know all about the outlaw bands. I've been wondering. Who was Stringer afraid of?"

Zanne was shocked.

"You're not suggesting Vanan could have anything to do with the outlaws? Why, that's ridiculous."

"*Oh!*"

With a fierce gesture, Dimen grabbed the stuff of her tunic.

"Zanne. Zanne, look at this. This hasn't been in a vault for hundreds of years. This is good Inland cloth. You're a weaver's daughter, you should know. *Don't you see—?*"

She broke off, looking around in fear for that solitary groom. Zanne was afraid herself that Chiro would come back and hear this wild outburst.

She said soothingly, "Dimen, I think you'd better calm down."

"Zanne, please don't do what that woman wants you to do."

"But, Dimen—it's the Daymaker. This what we left Inland for, don't you remember?"

"I don't care about the Daymaker," said Dimen slowly. "I—never did. I only came with you to protect you, Zanne. And I think I've failed."

Zanne shook her head kindly. "You don't mean that. You wanted to come. You know you did."

The servant returned and stood close by, watching them. Dimen was leaning against a pillar. She looked ill and weak.

Zanne knew what was wrong, although she didn't like to say so. Dimen was jealous. She had lost her magic, while Zanne remained powerful. She had no great task to perform, no destiny. And she was even losing her looks. Suddenly Zanne saw how ugly she had grown: dark skin turned greyish sallow, dull eyes; gaunt hollow cheeks and knobbly wrists. No wonder Chiro preferred a sturdy farmgirl. She felt almost repelled by this pathetic figure. But she tried not to show it.

"Poor Dimen. You don't belong here, that's the problem. You just can't survive—" she laughed "—without that old turnip-sprouting mumbo jumbo."

Dimen stared at her friend, amazed. Could this be Zanne speaking? For a moment she glimpsed the truth. But then it was gone again. She felt tired, very tired; that was all she knew. Zanne took her arm and led her off to their rooms, where she could rest quietly, with one of Vanan's servants close at hand.

Chiro and Vanan watched the two girls go by. They were in one of the storerooms. It was Vanan who had called Chiro away, deliberately leaving the guests alone.

"I don't like this," said Chiro. "It's going on too long. You should never have told her about the Hillen warding. You've scared her off."

Vanan's expression was less scholarly now. The lines of authority around her eyes and mouth had shifted somehow: rather unpleasantly.

"Patience," she told him. "She couldn't possibly get through the door without knowing who guards it. I don't want her to make her decision then. I want her to be *mine* before we make a single move. I do not take risks, Chiro. That is how we come to be here, instead of groveling in the

143

dirt outside chewing half-roasted mutton bones."

"But what about the other one?"

Vanan chuckled. She actually enjoyed Chiro's stupidity. He wouldn't be half so useful if he was more intelligent.

"Leave her to Zanne."

If Chiro had been patient for a little longer, they might have won the game. Vanan knew, of course—how could she not—that in certain ways the strong girl was weak and the weak girl strong. But Dimen's feeble but stubborn resistance didn't mean anything at all if she could destroy the friendship. And that process was almost complete. Unfortunately Chiro was getting restless. He found it hard to sit still and do nothing, so near such an enormous prize.

During the day, light entered the castle through many rows of small windows high in the walls. They were unglazed. The air that came in was not warm, though it was Sunfall now, the deep turning point of the year. Neither was it cold. The windstorm seemed to have died down at last.

Zanne stood under an array of windows, looking up. She was thinking (Dimen had achieved this much) that it seemed a long time since she had been out of doors. Longer still since she had seen the sun, or a blue sky. But even the bleak wasteland would be better than being cooped up indoors.

Chiro came quietly up the gallery. Though he was a big man, broad shouldered, he carried himself delicately. He always wore heavy riding boots, an odd contrast with his rich clothes; but he still managed to walk very softly. He stopped beside Zanne.

"What are you thinking?" His eyes were on her face with the usual flattering attention.

Zanne laughed.

"Nothing important. I'm thinking I can't seem to hear the wind any more."

He smiled. "You're right. The storm is over. Would you

144

like to go for a ride? We must find you some proper clothes."

Zanne had never used a saddle or bridle. She had never had special clothes for anything except in the sense of good ones for meeting and old ones for a dirty job.

"Oh—thank you."

Traveling had changed the stern covenanter. She had been *rich* since she entered the borderlands, and that fact had had an insidious effect. She had learned to value and to guard her property. She would not have thought it possible that Zanne of Garth could be corrupted by something so shallow as material possessions. But it was so. She had disdained the Roadkeepers' simple ostentation. But she liked living in Vanan's grand style.

They were alone in the gallery. Chiro took her arm and led her to an alcove, where there was a low ledge like a windowseat built into the wall.

"Yes, the storm is over, Zanne. But have you made up your mind? Do you want us to send you back to Fatland?"

Zanne looked away. She knew now why Vanan had been so careful not to press her. She wouldn't admit it to Dimen, still she realized this was a very big choice. People wouldn't understand. The Garth meeting, her mother, the Tecovs— they would call Zanne a Covenant breaker. She understood that. She was prepared. And yet it was hard to say the final word. It would be easier if Chiro didn't stare at her so hard.

"Dimen wants to go home," she said. "Can you arrange that? Can you see that she gets safely back to Fatland?"

Chiro's bright eyes just flickered.

"You want me to take care of her? Don't worry, I will. Vanan often leaves things like that to me."

She thought he was like a child—so eager to please.

"Are you afraid?" he asked laughingly. "Afraid of Hillen Coven?"

Zanne smiled.

145

"You don't understand. I am Hillen Coven."

Chiro looked, for a second, quite horrified.

"No—no. I'm Zanne of Garth. But the Covenant is in me, as much as in anyone. I meant—I make up my own mind."

She paused. She was thinking that Vanan and Chiro did *not* understand. Inland had been unjust to the past, and the power that was not magic. But that power—reborn—must not return the evil. It must be for everyone.

Chiro waited on her silence as long as he could bear it—not long. He leaned forward with a soft, sudden gesture and took her hands. He looked to right and left with practiced swiftness before he spoke, which was useless but involuntary.

"Are you thinking of Vanan?"

She did not understand him. She had never touched his hands before. The clasp was unpleasant, for no obvious reason. They were muscular hands, and implicit to her magic sense with some skill or trade she could not quite put a name to.

Chiro leaned closer. "There is so much power here," he breathed. "And only you can wake it, Zanne. Only you perhaps in the whole world. Don't start; Vanan says that. She doesn't often make mistakes, or we wouldn't be where we are. She's afraid of you. She doesn't mean me to know, but I can tell."

He squeezed Zanne's hands tighter. She still did not answer so he was forced to speak more clearly.

"Don't worry about Vanan," he whispered distinctly. "I can't touch her, it would be death for me to try. But you can break her. Then you will turn on the Daymaker. And we two will control the emf. The power that existed before magic, the power that built the towers of light. We'll rule together. We'll be so *rich*, Zanne—"

Zanne hardly noticed the strange word "electricity." She had just realized what was wrong with Chiro, why he was holding her hands so tightly. She was horribly embarrassed for him. But that didn't last more than a moment. Chiro was not really lovesick. Or rather, it wasn't really Zanne that he wanted.

"You've made a mistake, Chiro," she said slowly, withdrawing from his grasp. "I don't 'break' people. I wouldn't if I could."

He was so excited he did not see the disaster he had caused, but plunged on headlong.

"You think you haven't the power, that's what they teach in Fatland. But all power is one. Vanan knows. You could destroy her."

Zanne stared. She had only been disgusted with Chiro, for betraying Vanan. Now the whole horrible truth began to sink in. She remembered what Dimen had said. *Perhaps we did meet Vanan's people.*

Vanan the scholar, who lived in such luxury, in the middle of the outlaw infested wasteland. Who knew everything that "the bands" did, and didn't fear them at all. Her lieutenant, with his gold chain and his gold ring and good Inland cloth on his back.

The dream that Zanne had been living in for days suddenly fell away. Appalled and furious, she realized how blind she had been. How could she have been so taken in? She saw Vanan's face in her mind's eye. The hungry, hungry eyes, greedy for limitless power.

Stringer's chief.

And now she knew what trade it was, that she felt in Chiro's hands.

Zanne stood up. She wanted to be sick. She wanted to get out of these hateful fine clothes. Were they just stolen, or stripped from the dead body of another Inland girl? She wanted to scrub the taint of them off her skin.

"You are an assassin," she said. "And Vanan is worse. She's worse than the outlaws. They do the dirty work, she just takes her share."

"Zanne!" he cried. "What are you talking about? You're talking nonsense!"

But his protests came too late.

He had offered her an ugly partnership, but she knew better than that. Did he think she didn't understand that once the Daymaker was awake there would be no need for true magic here? If she had done what they wanted immediately, she and Dimen would probably be dead by now.

She was not afraid. She was far too angry for that. She turned on her heel and marched away from him.

Chiro didn't stir. On his face was a look of growing terror, as he realized what he had done. It was not Zanne he feared.

She walked down the gallery, then she hurried, then she ran. She did not look to see if she was followed. Dimen was not in her room. Dimen had known all along. She ran down the stairs, her heart thumping wildly. The big hall was empty. She didn't hesitate but ran on. Where could Dimen be? She ran into the stable yard. It was empty again: only three horses in the stalls. No sign of Dimen. Spirit lamps burned brightly. Suddenly she saw the barred gates. She made up her mind to shift that bar now, with true magic. She would pattern it into something movable. That was a good idea. Then there would be an escape route ready when she had found Dimen. She began to cross the yard. We'll take all three horses, she thought, her mind very clear. That will give us a start.

She did not reach the gate. Her muscles slowed, they would not obey her. Zanne sobbed. Horror, horror. She did not turn around. The body turned, with Zanne inside it.

Vanan stood in the doorway of the house. Dimen was

beside her. A thing was beside her, a puppet with invisible strings. Dimen's helpless eyes looked out of its face.

Then Zanne knew the worst. Her mind had been invaded. Not just now, but ever since she entered this place. Vanan had no true magic, but not no magic at all. She was like Stringer, who could "make you eat your own hand." But her evil power was far greater. How else had she come to rule over the bands? And Dimen had resisted, at least enough to know that her reason was being abused. But now even her resistance was over.

Chiro came running down the steps, the skirts of his robe flying. The sound of his boots crashed through the silence.

"They're trying to escape!" he cried.

She let him cross the yard halfway. Then the fine young gentlemen stumbled, and came to a halt.

"You child," said Vanan dispassionately. "Only a child believes its own lies. Did you think your fine clothes could hide what you are from a student of Hillen? It was only my magic that kept her deceived, right from the start. A place beside *you*—even on a throne? You'd have done better to threaten her with your knife."

Chiro walked stiffly, awkwardly up the steps and turned, so that Vanan was flanked by two puppets. His expression was that of a harnessed animal, responding sullenly to a tug on the accustomed halter.

Vanan smiled.

"So, it comes to an open contest. I thought it might. Perhaps Chiro has only saved me from a useless expense of patience. They told you, didn't they, Zanne, that there are two magics in the world. But they never told you that your 'power' is only the second and the weaker. The First Magic, the old magic, is the magic of the mind.

"Think, Zanne, when you were a little girl. Before they told you you must only talk to turnips and stones. Wasn't it much easier, more *natural* to speak to human minds? To make them see what you wanted them to see. To make them do what you wanted them to do .... That is the old, the deep, the real Magic...."

Zanne knew that the words were not just words. Vanan was using them in a way that was forbidden, like someone swinging an ax with dull repeated blows at a locked door. It was hard to resist. But not so hard as Vanan must have believed.

It couldn't really be true that Dimen had more resistance than Zanne. It couldn't be true that this Outland woman was better than Zanne, either. That was impossible. She had only been taken unawares. She called up her power—and felt it answer. She hid her triumph, but she knew she was no longer a puppet. She started to walk, slowly. It was like walking in a river, against a strong current.

Now she was standing by her friend. She took Dimen's hand, clasped it firmly.

"Come on, Dimen. I want to go home"

For a moment they stood in front of the woman who was doing her best to kill them, or worse, thinking of nothing but the warmth of renewed friendship.

"You were right," said Zanne ruefully. "As usual."

Dimen only looked at her sadly, and did not speak. Zanne was puzzled. Dimen ought to be proud and glad that Vanan was beaten. But this was no time to ask questions. Zanne began to lead her friend away, out of the evil power.

But Dimen was confused. She was trying to pull Zanne toward the stable gates. Zanne knew that was wrong. They had to go through Vanan's stronghold. There was a door somewhere in there. It was their only chance of escape.

"Come on, Dimen. Don't fight me. This way—"

Vanan never moved. She did not set her assassin on them. But Zanne understood the battle was not over. She must reach the door, the one she could see in her mind. Nothing must prevent her from opening that door.

It was very bright inside the building, brighter far than Zanne remembered it. Light flashed on the pale walls, somehow making it difficult to see the way. She walked quickly. Dimen was still trying to tug the other way. Her soft familiar voice scratched in Zanne's ears like the buzzing of an insect.

"Zanne, no. Stop. Not this way, turn back." But behind Dimen (Zanne knew without looking) Vanan stood in the corridor. To escape from Vanan it was necessary to run away from her. That was obvious. Why couldn't Dimen understand?

The shining walls were making pictures in Zanne's mind. She saw the cave of the makers burning, and the cruelty of the mob. And further back, little Zanne Townsend laughed at because she loved things that went up and down, things that went round and round. All she wanted was to wear shoes in summer, to eat white bread. But she couldn't even want these things. She must not. I hated Garth, thought Zanne. I've been trapped all my life. It's only in the Outland that I've been free.

Still behind her someone was tugging and whining. She looked back and saw Dimen somehow grown smaller, pulling on her wrist like a sulky toddler. She wants me to give in, thought Zanne. She's jealous.

Hadn't it always been so? All the way from Inland, Dimen holding back and complaining. Dimen Roadkeeper was always jealous. She only made friends with the little farmgirl so she could laugh at her. It was very hard to bear. Dimen hardly deserved to be rescued. Not that Zanne would leave her behind, even now. But it was impossible to keep on hauling against this dead weight. It wasn't fair, whatever the rules about forbidden things. Zanne couldn't endure it any

151

longer. With hardly a thought (it was so easy) she withdrew some of her powerful intention from the task of reaching that door. She turned it on the feeble, stubborn mind that was holding her back.

"Ah—"

In the stableyard, Vanan released her breath with a long satisfied sigh. Chiro, who was sitting on the steps now, looked up at his lady and quickly looked away. Nothing had happened, no time seemed to have passed. But he was frightened. He knew there was magic going on. In the middle of the yard the yellow-haired girl stood. She hadn't moved. Her eyes were turned inward, her face was more empty than the face of a corpse. Chiro shuddered.

Dimen could not move hand or foot. Vanan still held her. It was only in her mind that she was with Zanne in the shining passages. She saw them around her, a ghostly image laid over the stableyard, and she was there. Her hand ached and burned in Zanne's grip. She knew that she was joined to Zanne by the magic that was called "forbidden." Forbidden or not, it had given her a chance of saving her friend. But now—

She would not meet Vanan's triumphant glance. Two tears crept from under her lowered eyelids. The Holder of the First Magic laughed softly.

Dimen saw that Zanne would open the door that Vanan wanted her to open. When she woke from the trance she was in now, she would already be broken. She would be Vanan's creature. She would wake the Daymaker, and Vanan—this monster—would have control of the only kind of power she lacked: power over the material world, as well as over minds. Dimen still didn't understand just what the Daymaker might be. But she understood enough. And she could sense, beyond knowledge, a terrible threat to Inland.

She knew she was to blame. It was a sin and a shame to

love someone like Zanne of Garth and just sit back and enjoy the fireworks. Zanne needed someone who would pull her up sometimes and tell her the truth about her wild ideas. Poor Zanne, poor dear turniphead. What a mess she was in now. There was nothing Dimen could do. She could put up a fight against Vanan, but not against Vanan and Zanne of Garth together. She could feel Zanne now, battering on her mind, frighteningly strong. She could not hold on.

Then Dimen realized that she was not quite defeated. She could make no magic out of this place. Nothing would answer her. Not the unnatural relics of the past, or the tainted, exhausted earth itself. But there was one source she might draw on. Not easily, the way Zanne had lifted herself above the borderland; still, she might try it. At Hillen they told you: the body has its safeguards against the magic it carries. Do not on any account defy them, except in the last emergency.

It was a pity she was already tired. Ever since she left Inland she had been getting weaker, and now she was almost worn out. She remembered the forest, and the spirit of the wood who had come to them like a human woman, to wish them well. But she had given Chestnut's token away. She had no protection now.

Was this the last emergency? She could hardly believe that. It seemed so unlikely that Dimen of Mosden should be contemplating doing something heroic. Yet Zanne must be stopped, saved from herself. She thought of a boy called Eko, held him in her mind a moment, just in case her effort should succeed, and cost what it might cost.

She thought of the taste of preserved peaches, eaten with Zanne in the storm, in the shelter of that absurd little Junk.

*Very well, Vanan. I won't let you have her. I know you are stronger but I just won't let go. So now what are you going to do?*

153

Zanne opened her eyes.

But her eyes had never been closed; Zanne had been somewhere else, not looking out of them. She had been having a nightmare. There were shining walls, and a goal that seemed the most desirable thing on earth. Then suddenly it changed. The walls turned to knife blades. She was going to be cut to pieces. But Dimen was there holding her back. Dimen was fighting with someone, but she never let go of Zanne's hand.

Slowly the stableyard returned. She remembered what had been happening: the horrible moment when she knew her mind was not her own. The time since that moment was confused, though it had been so real. She thought she had been going to do something very bad. But Dimen had saved her. Dimen had saved them both.

She saw a puddle of rich, dark cloth, lying at the top of the yard steps. It took a moment for her to understand that that was Vanan.

She was gone. The monster was gone forever. There was nothing more to fear.

"Dimen!" cried Zanne, as relief flooded through her. "Dimen, you've beaten her! You're a heroine!"

But there was no answer.

Zanne did not see Chiro at all. She did not know that he ran away, white faced, leaving his lady where she had fallen. She went over to where her friend was lying. She took Dimen's hand. It was warm—but it was empty, empty as a discarded glove.

Zanne put her arms round her friend and lifted her until the shining dark head lay heavily on her shoulder.

"Dimen?"

In the light of the spirit lamps Dimen's face had changed. Zanne couldn't understand how she had ever thought Dimen ugly. But she looked older, somehow. Her eyes were closed, her mouth smiled quietly as if she was dreaming. But she was not asleep.

Zanne noticed suddenly how the stable yard smelled of Inland, of home. One of the horses heaved a sigh and shifted noisily in its stall. Dimen did not stir. Zanne stared at the still face—unable to believe.

She began to cry, holding Dimen and rocking her.

"No—it can't be," she sobbed. "We were going to be friends forever. We were going to get old...."

And Zanne had been in trouble before, but there had always been a way out, something that would make everything right again. She had thought the world was like that: it might frighten you but it would never really hurt you. She could not believe that this terrible thing had happened to Dimen, really happened and could not be undone.

She did believe it in the end. She stopped crying then, and just knelt there holding Dimen's body, shivering, for what seemed a very long time.

# CHAPTER 8

AT LAST SHE left Dimen and went into the building. There was no sign of Chiro. He must have fled to the wasteland. Zanne didn't think he would last long out there now that the source of his power was gone. She imagined that the pair had not been kindly rulers to their raider subjects. Chiro would pay for that now. As she walked past the storerooms that held the choicest booty from a thousand raids on Inland, she surprised two of Vanan's servants. They were hauling a huge bundle. They gaped at her and ran, stopped to look back with eyes no longer dull and blank but bright with excitement. They knew Vanan was dead (how could they not?). They did not seem to mourn her. One of the two even sketched a kind of bow.

"Lady—?"

Zanne shook her head, shuddering. The figures ducked out of sight. They would be back, to reclaim their plunder. In hours, perhaps, the "great house" would be stripped of all its treasure.

Everything was the same. The pale shining walls, the wide halls. But Zanne felt a change. There was a presence here that she had not perceived before. While Vanan hid the truth about herself and her confederate, she had hidden the truth about their home too. Zanne knew this place now. She knew where she was.

She climbed the stair to the first gallery, and followed a passage leading to the center of the building. She was aware that she was retracing her trance journey. It was not so bright now in here. The spirit lamps were few and guttering. Still she walked without hesitation, straight to the door. Chiro had shown it to her and Dimen: just one of the many mysteries of this ancient place. He must have enjoyed doing that. Or perhaps he really didn't know. Vanan probably never trusted him as much as he thought she did.

This was the door she would have opened for Vanan if Dimen had not prevented her. It was blank, without lock or bar. She stood for a moment, then lifted her hand and knocked.

"Come in," said a thin, high-pitched voice from behind the door that had been sealed for centuries.

Zanne pushed on the blank slab. It opened smoothly inward. She saw a huge room. Everything in it was white, white as the sun in winter. Great white blocks stood around the walls, more rose like islands from the floor. And every block had a dark face, and the eyes were all looking at Zanne. Not many creatures, she sensed; but one, behind all the eyes. Silently, silently waiting as it had waited for years.

In the shelter of one of the islands, someone was playing house. That was the first thought that came to Zanne. She saw the moonlamp that was lighting the room with its silver glow. She saw a little pallet bed, an earthenware stove, a curtain of canvas behind which could be glimpsed a neat washstand. An old woman with a nut-brown weatherbeaten face and a shock of white hair was standing beside these arrangements. On a railing by her bed hung a dark blue Hillen robe, much battered and travel-worn.

"Who are you?"

The old woman came forward, holding out a knobbly brown hand.

"Ido Covener. A covener without a meeting, covener of the roads and the wide world."

"How long have you been here? How did you get in?"

Ido chuckled.

"How did I get in? Oh, I have my ways. How long? There has always been a guardian. We always guard these places—often not in body, but I am an earthy creature. I need my flesh and bones with me."

She shook Zanne's hand, and waved around at her little holding.

"You see, I have reached water. And devised myself a most ingenious privy. One day, when the flowers grow here again, they ought to call it Ido's garden."

Zanne felt the hand in hers. It was hard and solid. And yet she knew it couldn't be. This room was sealed.

"Are you really here? *Only* here?"

Ido withdrew her hand, a trifle sharply.

"Hmmph! They didn't lie. One can't hide much from you, child. Still, you shan't have all the secrets all at once. Save something for your old age."

She chuckled again.

"I will admit though, that I know your name and why you are here. Hillen has been waiting anxiously—to see the end of Zanne of Garth's choice journey."

A little while ago, Zanne would have been angry to think that her teachers had been spying on her. Not now. They couldn't help but see what was in front of their eyes: which was to say, all Inland. She thought of this guardian, waiting helplessly. They knew what she meant to do, but no one had tried to stop her. They could not. They had forbidden themselves the means.

She thought of how completely she had been deceived, and her own strong will used against her. The poison Vanan had fed to her was gone now. Dimen was a loving friend

158

again, Garth was Zanne's dear home. But the other things were also real, and she had had no power against them. There was a Zanne who was greedy and arrogant, who hated Dimen. She would never be able to forget that now.

"It is true," she said. "The First Magic is older. It is stronger."

"Quite so," agreed Ido. "But what makes you so sure that older means better?"

She grinned cheerily.

"I prefer the new myself. And strength, as you well know, Zanne, is not always an advantage."

There was a short silence. Zanne looked around her. Her vision had cleared. There were no patient eyes on the white blocks, only desks of little buttons and numbers in red and black; and small gray windows into nothing. There was a silt of dust over the whiteness, but no other sign of decay. The Daymaker had survived well, sealed in its tomb. She had said she would be bound to know when she had reached her goal, because she had seen makers at Garth. There was nothing like those metal beasts here. But she knew.

"This is the Daymaker."

Ido nodded.

"The whole building is the Daymaker. The moving parts, as far as I understand it, are elsewhere. But this is the heart of the brute."

"Yes."

Zanne could feel that. Chiro and Vanan had been living in the Daymaker's front porch, like rats under the steps of a barn. She could sense beyond this hall and under it rooms they had never seen, full of strange presences. But it was all one. It was the mystery that had delighted her, in that ruin in the Garth valley. The laws of action, the principles behind

159

nature; taken out of the muddy world and set up on their own. The bright, bright motion she had loved all her life . . . .

"Was it really 'emf'?" asked Zanne. "The same as lightning. Or when you rub a bit of resin and it sticks to things?"

"The very same."

"But that's silly."

"To us. But in the other world, it was usable power."

"Why did no one *tell* me?"

"That is what children always say. If I tell you that your teachers consider it unwise to *call up the past* in any way, I suppose that will only make you angry again."

"I don't understand," whispered Zanne.

"It is quite simple, child. The journey is over. Now comes the choice."

If the makers operate, Inland is not. Magic dissolves, becomes something barely existing. Likewise, if Inland is to be real, the makers must be dead shells. Zanne had come a long way around, to understand what her mother said to her in Townsend kitchen. Now she could see. The world was like a picture, one of those pictures that can be a cup or a tree. Both patterns are there, but the picture cannot be both. It has to be one or the other.

Most people in Inland saw the Covenant picture only. The ones who couldn't accept that pattern ran away and became outlaws. It was Zanne's misfortune (so she called it now) to see both worlds, the magic one and the other that belonged in the past. And to love them both. To accept the makers and the rubbish that made Junk as being made of the same stuff as flowers. She could not help herself. It was as natural to Zanne as seeing color.

She crossed the floor and laid her hand on a sloping desk, among the buttons and the empty window-eyes. She felt her heart go out to the beauty of this power. She knew that she

160

could speak to the Daymaker and it would answer her. Her loving magic would heal the decay that she couldn't see, behind these faces. She could call back the other world, make its pattern rule again.

And unmake Inland.

There was no doubt in Zanne's mind. She knew what she was going to do. She had been learning, all the long road from Garth, that *there is no separate power*. Trying her own healing and holding in the border village, seeing what the outlaws did to the land around them. Nothing is free. The price always has to be paid.

The Daymaker was flawed, like the world of the past. Fatally flawed, because the people did not understand that simple fact. The strange laws of their world hid it from them, until it was too late and the towers of light fell in ruin. But oh, what beauty and brightness there had been in that maimed world. And how dull and small Inland looked beside it.

She wished she could just walk away. But that was not enough. Even sleeping, the Daymaker was dangerous. It was the past, undead. As long as it existed it would draw people like Vanan and the outlaws. And the land around it would remain ruined and empty. As long as places like this remained, Inland could not grow.

"There is not enough good magic," she whispered.

"Perhaps not," answered Ido's voice behind her. "But if at first you don't succeed in doing something the right way, it is no kind of improvement to try and do it the wrong way instead."

One world, or the other. Zanne stood looking at the Daymaker. She forgot about Ido. She was all alone now. She tasted salt on her mouth, and didn't know until then that she was crying.

She remembered the barnyard of some neighbor's farm.

Another little girl giggling as they crouched in hiding; and Zanne's mother leading out the beast that was to be killed, a sheep or maybe a bull calf. Arles never frightened the animal. It looked up at the covener as she spoke. It trusted her, it knew it was safe.

How could Mother do that? How could she stroke the poor beast, hold it in her arms, and then kill it?

Zanne swallowed her tears. She could not cry now. She had to be a covener, if ever in her life. There was no one else to be with the Daymaker, and give it the good death it needed. She moved from face to face, steadily and surely, laying her hands on each of the white desks in turn. There was no effort in what she did. And yet she knew that she was using, for the first time in her life, her whole talent. This was work. All the rest had been child's play.

*Don't blame me, sister/brother. I will die too.*

And as she walked the wide floor, she was saying good-bye, finally, to something bright and rare. In her mind's eye she saw again Uncle Lol going over the hill with the sunlight on his hair. Somewhere in Zanne a little girl had always been waiting. Hoping always that her uncle Lol would come back, with his tricks and his treats that never had to be paid for. It was gone, gone forever, the world of lights and colored fire and sugar candy. She would never be that child again, not even in her dreams.

But in her heart, for the great Maker and herself, she held the candle flame.

It was done. Zanne sat down at the doorway again, where steps descended to the floor. The Daymaker's heart chamber had been silent when Zanne entered it. There was no word for the increase of silence now.

She laid her head on her knees. She was utterly empty and desolate.

Ido came and sat down beside her.

"Oh, why did it have to be me? I loved it so—"

"That is exactly why, Zanne."

The old woman glanced at the dead faces, for which she felt all the disgust a normal Inlander has for such things. But she suppressed her relief at the monster's death, to comfort Zanne.

"We must love what we destroy, child. Otherwise we could not destroy it properly, and we would only release more evil. That is why the Daymaker has waited so long. In that other world a place like this meant a very great deal to the people, though they never thought of it. It carried its meaning into our time, changed into our terms. So it remained a place of power, almost immune to time and decay. Only great magic could do away with such a creature. And no one before had had enough magic, Zanne—with enough love to make it safe."

She patted Zanne's shoulder.

"And now perhaps we'd better get back to your friend."

Zanne looked up. She had not forgotten. No. It had only been possible to leave the stable yard, to remember the Daymaker at all, because what had happened to Dimen must not be for nothing.

"My friend is dead."

She wished she had not spoken. Now it was real. Ido Covener nodded. Her eyes looked into Zanne's without pity, but with great kindness.

"I am eighty-seven years old," she remarked. "And yet I believe the call when it comes will still seem too soon."

She gave Zanne's shoulder a little shake.

"Now don't be greedy for more blame than you have earned, Zanne of Garth. We have only to deal with What Is, remember; not what might have been. Your friend died bravely, doing her right work. Let us wish for the same luck ourselves when our time comes."

She got to her feet and drew the girl up beside her.

"Listen to me, Zanne. The road will be long, but we will find our way. And this time when we can make night into day, and all those other marvels; it will be true control: of the whole pattern, losing nothing along the way. So don't you despair, Zanne. And don't ever be ashamed of that love of yours. For now, we must say good night. But we will be back."

They left the chamber then, with its door standing wide open to time, and the dust, and the wasteland's scavengers.

Ido went looking for the servants, the ones who hadn't already fled. She organized them into an escort. They were quite willing, even disappointed to find the new mistress was leaving. Dimen's body was carried on a sled, horse drawn; the kind used by the scavenging parties. And so they left the Outland, traveling straight along one of the old roads. They met no raiders or any other obstacle. But whether that was luck or due to Ido's magic, Zanne did not know.

A half moon after the destruction of Vanan, Zanne and Dimen came back to the forest settlement in the sweet chestnut glade.

Sunfall had passed. It was Leafall, the harvest month. Zanne knelt by a grave not far from the foresters' cabins. There was no stone or ornament; that wasn't the Inland way; only the green grass carefully replaced. The forest covener had not said a word of blame. To these people, living so near the borderlands, death in a fight with the raiders was not such a shocking thing. She died well—that was all anyone had to say.

Zanne was crying, but she wiped her eyes. She had been told she must not be greedy for blame. She was very humble just now, and only wanted to do as she was told.

"No—I won't hate myself," she said, aloud. "That won't do you any good, will it, Dimen? But I will remember. All my life you will be with me. Whenever I am happy. And whenever I need you too—telling me that I'm being a prig, and arrogant and blind ...."

"Good night, Dimen. Sleep well."

It was late in New Spring. The hawthorn hedge around Garth Inn's garden was freshly covered in bright and tender green, with knots of maybuds clustered under the leaves. Cowslips and snakeheads nodded on the Green, ladysmock and marsh marigolds were opening down by the river. A wagon drew up outside the inn. One passenger got down. She spoke quietly to the wagoners as she took her box, and then the oxen slowly hauled their charge through the gate into the innyard. Some children who had been playing on the steps of the Garth Inn came running out. They stared shyly. This girl was almost grown up, and she wore town clothes. She smiled at them. They giggled, pondering whether or not it was a stranger; but as the passenger did not speak they lost interest and returned to their game.

A tall man with a brown beard came out of the inn door. He stood considering, as if he too was wondering whether this was a stranger. Then she turned and saw him and flew like a bird into his arms. Zanne had come home.

She walked up the valley beside her father, sometimes holding his hand, sometimes leaning and rubbing her face against his jacket sleeve. Hurst carried his daughter's box on his shoulder. He did not speak much, only a little, mildly, of her journey and of the pretty weather. It had been a good year so far for the farmland.

Over their heads was the blue vault of the sky, with white clouds hanging like flowers in the clear air. On either side the fields were just springing blue green, gray green, in rows of wheat and barley. From the hedge a yellowhammer sang—*a little bit of bread and no cheese!*—flying before them from one high twig to another, its yellow dapple head bobbing as the breeze rocked the branches. And beyond that all the birds were singing. The lambs that had not yet gone up to the downs cried out in high-pitched bleats, and their mothers answered them gruffly. In the hedgebanks of the Garth road that Zanne knew almost flint by flint, chalk puddle by chalk puddle, there were early orchids with spotted leaves: stitchwort, dog violets, yellow rattle, and wild arum.

She walked as if in a dream. When she was a child and people said the Garth valley was beautiful, she had agreed cheerfully. All she really knew was that it was familiar. It was home, so it must be beautiful if beautiful was a compliment. Now she saw the loveliness, from this hedgerow crowded with flowers to the dear and perfect curve of the sheep downs across the sky. But she saw it through a veil: a barrier like shadowed glass. Dimen was dead. And Zanne had done things and suffered things that could not be wiped away. If you once leave Inland, you will never get back again. You can walk in the fields and woods; you can delight in their beauty. But you can never undo that journey. If someone had told Zanne that, almost a year ago, would she have listened? Would it have stopped her? No, it would not. Only this Zanne, on the other side, could see what that Zanne was doing. A child cannot be warned of how it will feel to have left childhood behind.

At the gate at the bottom of home meadow Hurst laid Zanne's box on the wall. He hugged her and held her away, looking ruefully and tenderly into her changed face. There had been letters through the winter; he knew all the story.

"You must have had a hard time getting out of those badlands," he said.

"No. It was all quite easy. Ido took care of everything."

Zanne and Ido had stayed in the forest for a while, and then they had returned to Hillen. Both the foresters and Hillen Coven treated Zanne with great respect. It was not only that the Daymaker was gone. Vanan's death was also important. The raiding bands would fight each other now until a new pair of leaders emerged. Mid-Inland could look forward to peaceful winters, for a while.

When she had been back at Hillen some days, Zanne was summoned to Holder Elima's study.

She stood in the familiar room, wearing again the olive smock and leggings of a Hillen student. They were her own clothes and still fitted her, but they felt very strange.

She was glad of this summons. She had not been comfortable, waiting to learn her fate. She had been given a room alone in Flores; which reminded her of the worst night of her young life, all those ages ago. The Tecovs had all been frighteningly kind. In the great hall none of her old friends seemed to know her. Girls came up and said a few words about Dimen, and then sneaked away. Or else they stared and whispered. It would have been hard to bear—but schoolgirls couldn't hurt Zanne now.

She stood with her head down, waiting to hear her sentence.

The moonlamp light glimmered on Elima's hair, finding a little more silver than when Zanne had first met the Holder of Inland.

"Well, my girl. You are very young to begin your life's work. But there is not much more that Hillen can teach you."

Zanne looked up.

"We are going to make you a covener," explained Elima.

Zanne stared. "Oh, no—"

Holder Elima raised her eyebrows.

"I don't want to be a covener. I'm not fit—"

"I think you must allow Hillen Coven to be the judge of that."

167

Zanne swallowed hard. She remembered it was not her business now to question and rebel. She had done enough of that.

"Am I allowed to say where I want to be placed?"

"You may ask."

"Then send me to the borderlands. Let me be covener of that village where we stayed. Where I was ill and Dimen looked after me."

She had decided, if by any chance she was allowed to continue her training, that was the work she wanted to do. To help those sly and miserable borderers, to share their poverty.

Holder Elima shook her head. She looked amused.

"We cannot send you there. And if we could—do you think it would be fair? To give those unfortunate people a covener who regarded her placing as a punishment? No, Zanne. I'm afraid it is worse than that. We cannot send you to the borders because you are needed elsewhere. Rare talents must not be wasted. There are other Daymakers."

Zanne looked at the Holder. She had wanted to be punished. Yes, this was bad enough. It was all she was fit for, with her marred, unnatural power.

"Yes," she muttered. "Yes, I see. Thank you, Holder."

"Zanne."

The Holder got up from her desk. The girl was halfway to the door, forgetting to wait until she was dismissed.

"Zanne, what did Ido tell you? You have no need to be ashamed of what you are. Be ashamed of arrogance, and of carelessness. But understand this. That strange double vision of yours—your love and understanding of the makers—is nothing other than true magic itself. It is the faculty that will make you, Zanne, one of the greatest coveners Inland has ever known."

Zanne of Garth turned back. Her face was puckered and

168

puzzled, like a child about to cry.

"Me?" she asked disbelievingly.

"Yes, you."

Elima laughed. She could see it was too soon, too soon by years, for Zanne to understand just what she was.

"Enough," she said, as if to the homesick baby of six years ago. "Go back to the hall. And please, try to be kinder to the other students. Everybody wants to praise you, but you are frightening them to death with your awesome looks."

Zanne worked very hard for the next two months. Then after Year's End she went to Mosden, to the Roadkeepers, a new-made covener. She had nothing to offer them in place of their daughter except this: herself. It was a difficult time, very sore for the grief that had just begun to heal. The Road-keepers' way of mourning was sometimes strange to a child of Garth. It took the form of dinners with crowded tables, of endless receptions and calls on Mosden worthies. All of them wanted to speak at length to Zanne, the friend of the heroine who had given her life in defense of Inland.

Zanne did not mind this version of the story. It wasn't hard enough on Zanne herself, but it was certainly no less than the truth. And it was comforting to hear her friend praised. Sometimes Dimen seemed very near—laughing and whispering wicked comments. But praise addressed to herself made her simply angry. She had told everyone: she loved the Maker, she only killed it because she had to. There was no virtue involved.

Now she was free. The Roadkeepers had other children. In time it might even be more comfortable for them to have a brave dead daughter than to have a living one mixed up in the awkward untradelike business of the Covenant.

Hurst put his daughter's small box down on the kitchen table. New Spring sunlight filled the room with its uncertain warmth, but the sunstove was still burning: a dull glow buried deep in the earthenware.

"Your mother's out hedging," he explained apologetically. "It's been so warm, you see, the season's got ahead of us. The job needed finishing—"

"I'll go to her," said Zanne.

It was a Garth welcome, not a town one, and she was glad. Under the Covenant all places are the same. Why should I stop work to rejoice that you've come home? (said her mother, through the empty kitchen). You have never been away, my daughter.

They were working up at the top of Townsend, where the Garth road turned right angles on itself and trotted away to Threetrees: steep open pasture above and fields below. Zanne saw them as she came across the hill: her mother and Bren and a girl who turned out, as she approached, to be Loyse, daughter of Liat the potter of Bine End. Up here the leaves were not so far advanced. It was an old hedge, almost as wide as Zanne was long. The main part was beech, but there was hawthorn and ash, and elder already fully out and little use for anything; and common roses and sweet briar not so much wild (as the hedgers used to say) as savage. The three were dressed in dun and brown. They wore sacking aprons and heavy rawhide gloves up to the elbow. You would have thought they were part of the hedge. But they were ruthless with themselves if it was so, slicing and stripping and twisting the branches into a long complex pattern.

When Bren saw Zanne he dropped his tools at once. He jumped down into the road as she came through the field gate opposite, pulling off his glove, and shook her hand grinning and blushing. Loyse came up behind equally eager. Zanne set her jaw. She only hoped this "fame" would wear off soon.

Arles rescued her. Together they walked down the road a little way, to where the bank sloped less steeply and they could sit looking over Garth. The blossoming clouds had massed together and acquired a strangely lovely shade of indigo. It began to rain. Arles put a sack with one of its long seams opened over her head, and handed another to Zanne.

"I won't be going back to Hillen," said the girl at last. "They told me not. I won't be going to college either. I'll never be a teacher now.'

"Yes, Zanne, I know. You have other work to do."

"I am sorry, mother."

Arles reached out—and drew back, as if she had remembered this was not her child any more. This was a young woman, seasoned in danger and hard won self-knowledge. She looked down the valley.

"Zanne, when you were ten years old your father and I knew this would come. I don't say we didn't hope you would find a way after all to be the covener in the next valley, to stay safe and near. But we were ready. You have brought us grief and sleepless nights in the last year, and no doubt there will be more. Don't worry, you are worth it, my darling. You will always be our dear daughter, wherever you go."

The spring rain sheeted over the fields below. It fell through sunlight and shadow with a musical sound, waking sweet scents from the earth and the new leaves. Zanne looked at her mother, who sat back on her heels with her hands loosely clasped on her sacking apron. The yellow hair that strayed out from under her country waterproof had strands of gray. Arles' cheeks were beaten red brown with a color that no longer faded out in the winter. She looked what she was: a countrywoman, a farmer, getting into middle age. But she held this valley in the palm of her hand. Zanne wondered why she had ever been sent to Hillen. What

171

was there to learn about magic that this woman could not teach?

She had had the chance to be a covener of her mother's kind. But she had wanted more. Something exciting, something no one else could see. Now it was too late. She would not have the farm or the town or the sun-dappled quietness of Hillen. She would go out into the world, a wanderer with no place of her own. And her work would be destruction not creation. Hillen Coven had told her so. One Daymaker was gone. But there were other Outlands, other makers. They needed Zanne too, to give them covenanted death. Rare talents must be used.

"I don't want to go!" she cried. "I want to stay in Garth!"

At last Arles held out her arms, and Zanne wept like a baby on her mother's shoulder. But only for a little while. The older woman looked into her daughter's tear-stained face.

"Ah," she sighed. "You remind me of someone, Zanne."

Arles stood up.

"I've got to get back to work," she said gently. "But see— I have a present for you."

She had brought a long stave away with her from the hedging. Now Zanne saw it was a traveler's staff, of sleek golden-gray ash wood, with the foot shod in bronze.

Along Townsend top-end the work went on: splitting and splicing and twining the unwilling branches, where the spring sap was flowing. Loyse began to whistle and Bren began to sing, in the still uncertain tenor of his young manhood. After a chorus or two his mother joined in. But Zanne sat under the hedgerow, which would be her house; and the rain, which would be her companion, now seeped in chilly drops through the sacking. She was thinking of the person of whom her mother had been reminded. A yellow-haired, gray-eyed girl. Who wanted everything, who wanted to change the world; and probably suffered for it. She had had her own choice journey once, and maybe it was long and hard. But in the end it brought her home.

So thought Zanne. And then the staff in her hand felt like a promise, not a sentence. There would be journey's end someday, with years to live the summer life of Inland.

Meanwhile, the white road stretched before her.

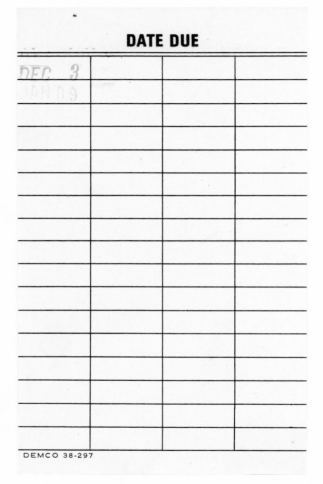

| DATE DUE | | | |
|---|---|---|---|
| DEC 3 | | | |
| JAN 09 | | | |
| | | | |
| | | | |
| | | | |
| | | | |
| | | | |
| | | | |
| | | | |
| | | | |
| | | | |
| | | | |
| | | | |
| | | | |
| | | | |
| | | | |
| | | | |

DEMCO 38-297